OWNED BY THE HITMAN

ALEXIS ABBOTT

PATHFORGERS PUBLISHING

Want to keep up to date with all my new releases, sales, and giveaways? What about getting a **Free** bad boy romance novel? Subscribe to my VIP Reader List:

http://alexisabbott.com/newsletter

IVAN

*J*ust one more hit, and the night is mine.

Of course, that's easily said. But a hit is not always easy. It takes calm and composure when the world is chaos, when any one little thing can go wrong and send the whole mess spiralling out of control. It takes control over your actions, a steady hand, the death of anxiety, because worry does you in every time.

For those reasons, and more, amateurs tend to do a hit from far away. Or if they don't have the equipment to snipe someone from a distance, they haul out a gun, fire like crazy, then run in a mad dash to get away.

I've never done a sloppy hit like that, not about to start now.

This guy I'm after is too good for that to work anyhow. He's either always flanked by bodyguards, or in the middle of a crowd. I know this because I've been following him for weeks. Planning my move. He's good, shakes things up, not much of a fixed schedule, but like all men with power, this guy has his vices. Vices he doesn't even trust his own body-guards to keep quiet.

For the third time this week, I walk behind him as he makes his way through a busy crowd down the street. This guy -- a trumped up millionaire from Florida who made his fortune selling coke to college kids, who enforced his reign by brutally beating punks who couldn't pay, and is now here in my city, offing people left and right -- he deserves to die.

He's balding, even though he's only in his thir-ties. A life of constant paranoia will do that to you, stress you out. But at this point I'm just annoyed he's dragged my ass around New York for weeks, doing my best to look inconspicuous, to blend in and not seem like I was watching. I'm sick of this shit stain, and ready to wipe him clean from the city.

So as he slipped out the back of the Italian mob owned deli and heads through the crowds down a side alley, I'm grateful.

I can finally end this.

But the alleyway is barely five car lengths long, a gun won't do here. No, I have to go in personal.

My black shoes are shiny, fancy looking. But they're quiet. And for a moment, we're just two well-dressed men taking a shortcut to any passerby. But my window of opportunity is narrow.

My heart skips a beat, and it's like time slows.

I'm gonna kill you, you son of a bitch.

But I can't hurry. Smooth steps, my hand reaching into my charcoal grey coat. And out comes the knife. It doesn't gleam, doesn't glisten. This one is a dull colour, but sharp. So sharp.

I close in on my prey, but he's a canny guy, and he detects me, his head twisting about.

But I'm better than him. And it's too damn late anyhow.

His turn only helps me, and I grab him about the mouth, his cries silenced. Now I gotta end this fast, before some person on either side of the alleyway walks by and notices us.

My knife slices through the air, and while I know it'll make a mess of my coat, that's the price to pay. The other options are too risky. I could stab him in the chest, but then he could block me, and though he's stocky and overweight, he might have hidden strength that could mess up my blade's arc.

The throat? Fuck, that's for amateurs. A killer like me knows when you slice a man's throat open, it's a noisy affair. Blood gurgling sounds would fill the alleyway, his dying cries drawing all sorts of attention.

So instead, I go for the heart. Right between two of his ribs I plunge that blade, and I sink into his left ventricle. I know it, because I've done it before. Because I can feel the way the blade moves through that muscular flesh of a man's heart.

This thug tries to cry out, tries to struggle away, but my blade slices clear through the center of his heart and into the right atrium.

He's done.

All that's left to do is to shift his body beside the dumpster, into the pile of trash bags. I can't rush, even though at this point every moment puts me at risk of being caught a murderer. I hold his mouth shut until he's completely limp, then dump him among the garbage.

Just another piece of trash.

The knife's no use to me now. I can never use it again, because it'd tie me to this killing, so I leave it in him. I look down and see that the blood spurt stained my grey overcoat, and that's what I'd expected.

Two grand down the drain.

I slip the coat off me, casually, as if it was just getting too warm for it, and I carry on down the alleyway. I wrap the coat up with my gloves and dispose of both a few blocks down the road in a Salvation Army donation bin.

They'll probably wash the evidence clean and sell it to someone in no time.

But I'm done now. Another cold kill finished.

I need a drink and a woman.

KATY

I can't bring myself to listen to another word the guy sitting next to me is saying, and I have to restrain every muscle to hold back the impulse to throw my drink in his face.

We're sitting in the VIP lounge of my own club, and not even the lavish orange tapestries my father decorated the round room with can distract me from the yuppies seated around me. They're a bunch of businessmen, and they rented the suite for the evening, so it's my duty as the Amber Room's owner to stop in for a chat.

Of course, that was before I realized these sleaze-bags are trying to buy the place out.

I know I don't look like the most intimidating person in the world.

My one-piece dress hugs my frame, sleek and black in the lounge's pale light, and my rich brown hair spills down over my shoulder in curls. The pearls wrapped around my wrist slide down my arm as I twirl my hair around my fingers.

At this point, that's all I can do to contain my agitation.

My dress feels hot, and the small room feels even smaller than it is with these creeps crowding it.

"So," the guy leaning uncomfortably close to me drones on, "if you consider the property values' change over the past few years, Ms. Foss — can I call you Katy? — there's a clear downward trend for establishments like this one, possibly thanks to mob activity."

"Uh-huh," I mutter dismissively, standing up and attempting to excuse myself silently.

"So there really isn't a better time to sell while you still can, and if you would just take a look at our offer—"

I'm already halfway to the door.

"Of course, gentlemen," I wave my hand, resisting the urge to refer to them as 'stooges,' "leave the paperwork on the table. I'll have a few drinks brought your way, hm? Do enjoy the evening, and don't be a stranger to the dance floor, won't you?"

I hear a couple of them trying to get a word in edgewise, but I'm already out the door and heading down the short hallway to the club floor, to my relief.

The nerve of them.

Ever since I inherited this night club from my father, it's been more and more trouble. I'd had to learn the ropes of managing the place to keep it from going under in the first few months.

Between staffing and accounting, it's a wonder I even have the time to entertain patrons like the suits in the VIP room behind me.

I certainly haven't had the time to redecorate the place.

The Amber Room. Dad had been going for a nod to all the local Russians, I guess. He once showed me a picture of some Tsar's famous palace in St. Petersburg that had an amber look about it. I push the door to the crowded dance floor open and get a reminder of his artistic vision yet again.

The place looks like a furnace.

Marigold-colored tapestries hang from the walls of the rectangular room, and the floodlights along the walls cast an amber light across the dance floor. Tawny booths line the side walls, and two couches stand on the elevated platform I step out onto.

The bar is at the far end of the room, near the exit. Between me and the stiff drink I desperately need, there's a sea of patrons dancing to the thrumming music the DJ is playing.

I plunge into the crowd without a seconds thought and navigate the floor with ease.

There are eyes on me as I make my way to the bar, I can feel them. They don't last long, though. I

ALEXIS ABBOTT

have an air of authority to the way I walk. I made sure to learn that walk early on.

It was the only way to not get swept up in the noise of the crowd. I don't get lost in it, I keep above it.

But the baggage of this place gets heavy.

I reach the bar and get the bartender's attention, holding up two fingers. She nods and promptly starts to pour my Jameson. It's a little quieter here, thanks to the room's acoustics.

Natalie, the bartender, knows what the look on my face means: a drink, right now.

"Everything alright, boss?" she chimes, sliding the drink over to me, happy for the break from the regular patrons.

I take a drink in response. "The VIPs are realty sharks. Nothing unusual."

She frowns, glancing towards the lounge door.

"Fuckers. Well hey, take it easy the rest of the night, eh? You've been working your ass off all week, you could use a little unwinding."

That gets a smirk from me. "Yeah? And do what, sit at home worrying about this place?"

Natalie rolls her eyes. "I dunno, but I know who might have a few ideas."

"Oh? Who's that?"

"The stud who walked in while I was pouring your drink and hasn't taken his eyes off you since."

I flutter my eyes as I process what she just said,

and before I can say "Wait—!" Natalie moves off to see to another patron, a wicked smirk on her face.

I turn my eyes towards the club entrance to brace myself for whoever she was talking about.

There are at least half a dozen men making their way into the club, but that's normal at this time of night. But amid the douches in popped collars tracking in the smell of too much cologne, there's one figure towering over the rest, and the dark blue eyes that catch my gaze tell me he's the one Natalie meant.

My heart jumped in my chest, but not because I was taken by the looks of the stranger. I turn my head before getting a better look at him beyond his tight-fitting gray suit and a teal tie.

For all I know, he could be a friend of one of the jerks in the lounge showing up late to the party. In fact, I decide that's exactly what he is.

I shoot Natalie a rueful look, to which she rolls her eyes with a playful smirk before I down the rest of my drink and spin around on the barstool to get up and make my way onto the dance floor, the clicking of my heels muffled by the music.

I don't flirt with patrons.

Natalie would tease me about it all the time, egging me on to "Live a little, Katy! You own a night-club, that's basically a free pass on all the ass in town!"

But that's the point, I remind myself as I start

dancing with some of the patrons, putting a fake smile on my face while the drunken crowd is cheering the DJ on.

I'm the club owner.

In case something goes down, I need to be on my toes all the time. What the businessman in the lounge said offhandedly about the local mob put a rancid, all-too-familiar taste in my mouth.

I can't afford to let my guard down in this kind of business. And that means no doing shots with the hot celebs that pass through my little club every blue moon.

The crowd gives me some cover for a while — the rich, young crowd is here in force tonight. Some of the wealthiest young adults in Brighton Beach are grinding against each other, right here on my dance floor.

A few semi-familiar faces try to get my attention as I pass by them, but I can hardly tell what's coming from whom, even as I try to listen for potential trouble.

"Oh my God, Katy, where did you get this euro-trash DJ? Love it!"

"Katy! The guy in the purple shirt is a scout for that modeling agency, help me get his number!"

"You would not believe what went down at the game tonight, did you see it?!"

There it was.

I shout a few distracted replies as I sneak off the

dance floor and ease myself down onto one of the couches lining the walls, just as the music starts to die down enough that I can hear myself think.

Where there were big, excited, drunken crowds this time of year, big sports games were usually responsible. I don't keep up with them, but I know games usually mean three things:

One happy crowd, one angry crowd, and a lot of bets on both side. Only one of those is good for my club, and I don't like those odds.

Although, I have to admit, even as I'm texting the bouncers to keep an eye out, I can't help but glance around the room and think I've lucked out and gotten the winning team's afterparty. All I see are giddy faces tonight, for a change.

But then my eyes pan across a familiar face in a gray suit heading my way, and I curse, lowering my eyes to my phone and twirling my hair nervously. Why did I have to leave the crowd?

I can feel him getting closer, and just as I lift my head to tell him I'm very busy and can't talk right now thank-you-very-much, I yelp as I realize he's already towering over me.

"Heart-shaped face and eyes like the sea? I think you outshine your own club."

His voice is deep, and it carries over the now-dull music with natural authority — there's a faint accent in it I can't place, but it only makes the attention he commands all the more soothing.

His jaw is chiseled, outlining a clean-shaven face that's only marred by the crease of his dimples as he gives an easy smile with full lips. His nose is straight but wide, offsetting soft eyes that are as soothing yet commanding as his voice. His short, light brown hair is clean-cut, making the imposing figure look like a statue come to life.

Up close, I realize that his tight-fitting suit is covering a powerful physique, even as he leans casually against the side of the couch I'm sitting on, arms folded like he's as relaxed as ever. I can just barely make out the edges of what might be a tattoo on his forearm, something without any immediate significance to me.

Color rises to my cheeks as I realize I've been staring at him blankly for a few moments, taken off-guard by his looks.

Not the kind of guy I was expecting. Not by a long shot.

"And who says I own this place?" I say, marshalling my composure again and crossing my legs, letting my hair dangle to the side as I tilt my head in curiosity, my gaze level.

"Your bartender is chatty," he explains, his face splitting into a grin. The lines on his face tell me he smiles a lot. "She said you were hoping I'd say 'hello' before the party gets worked up again."

I sit back, turning my chin up at him and letting a smirk play across my features. "Oh, did she? Maybe I ought to pay her a little more to keep her lips tighter."

I uncross my legs and lean forward, looking at him a little less playfully. "Look, if you're here with the realtors, you can tell your buddies in the VIP lounge to hit the road, if they didn't get the message."

He arches a thick but neat brow. This guy takes good care of himself, I notice.

"Not sure who you're talking about, but if you're hiding from them out here, they don't sound like VIPs, do they?"

I open my mouth, then close it again as I feel a blush in my cheeks again, and I cover my face with my hand, laughing at myself embarrassedly.

"Oh my God, I'm so sorry!" I rub my temple with my fingers, "I...I don't know what to say, it's been a stressful night."

"Seems so," he laughs, "I know you can't exactly choose between 'business or pleasure' here, but you seem tense. You shouldn't let a night like this go to waste, you know."

There's a playful glint in those eyes, dusky blue like a smoke-filled sky, and I realize that he's daring me. To do what, though?

As the dance music starts to pick up again and he gives a sideways nod to the dance floor suggestively, I get the message, biting my fingernail with a thoughtful smile on my face as my eyes rove over him.

Maybe Natalie's right, for once.

Besides, those lips are starting to make me curious.

I get my last chance to decide to be a responsible adult as he offers me a hand to draw me up, and before I realize what I'm doing, I've set my own slender hand into his, and a strong, gentle grip is lifting me to my feet and pulling me towards the dancers.

Whether it's the drinks or the atmosphere tonight, I immediately feel like there's a weight off my shoulders as I start dancing with the stranger.

He knows how to move in a suit, and his motions are every bit as limber and flexible as his demeanor hinted at. It's easy to read a man by how he carries himself.

I dance close to him, used to moving as well as one can in heels, and I feel his strong hands moving up my sides before long. And I revel in it.

It's been so long since I've let myself just have fun. In the back of my mind, I remember one more time that I'm barely scraping by, Dad's old debts are due soon, not to mention the *protection money*, and this place can't exactly watch itself.

Then I tell that part of my mind to take a night off.

Soon I'm grinding into the guy, the freeing atmosphere of the night urging me to enjoy this stranger's body, and as my wide eyes meet his, I realize he's been daring me into this from the moment he walked in.

It's in his moves as well as his gaze. He's always stepping to the side, a hand teasing at mine to follow, not just pulling me around but hinting for me to let him take the lead. With every moment that passes in the deafening music, I realize I want that more than anything else right now.

His eyes keep flitting to the exit with a meaningful look. I know exactly what he's hinting at, but my playful smile keeps him from thinking I'll go so easily.

By the time the song comes to a close, my backside is pressing into his front, and I feel powerful arms wrapping around me, those luscious lips whispering into my ear now that I can hear him speak.

"For someone so tense, you're in tune with your body. That's a rare pairing."

"I was about to say the same," I answer, exposing my neck to him and letting his cheek brush against it.

"So," he adds, hands moving down my sides to rest on my hips, and I can feel the desire in them. "The question is: are you willing to listen to what your body wants?"

I turn my head just enough for my gaze to catch his, and I bite my lip, a sparkle of my own in my eyes as I let the question linger in the air between us for a moment longer.

KATY

*L*ess than an hour later, I'm pressed up against him as we push through the door to his apartment, my hands tearing at his shirt while my lips are devouring his.

I hardly paid attention to where exactly we'd gone — we were all over each other on the taxi ride here. All that catches my eye is that it's an upscale penthouse not too far from the club.

He leads me through the richly-furnished living space to his bedroom, a platform bed with rich, cream-colored sheets waiting for us as I work his tie off and tear at the buttons of his shirt while his jacket slides off.

I've already kicked my shoes off, and his hands are working my dress down my body, feeling my slender frame as they go. My underwear isn't nearly as fancy as I'd like, but then again, I never expected to be going home with anyone when the night started.

But I can't concentrate on that, because the man's shirt is off now, and I can't help but stare at him as my mouth opens involuntarily.

His body isn't just strong, it's impossible.

Muscles that ripple down his arms meet at massive, rock-hard pecks that I brush my fingertips against in awe, not paying attention to what he's doing with my bra until I feel it fall to the floor and my breasts spill out before him.

The desire I see in his eyes drives me wild, my heart trying to pound its way out of my chest. I press myself against him, wrapping my arms around his neck as I feel the bulge in his pants pressing against my waist. His own heartbeat feels just as hard.

"I need this tonight," I breathe, need in my voice as I grind my hips into him. I let my hands slip down from his shoulders and slide to his washboard abs, biting my lip. "God, how are you even real?"

There's a smile on his face as his hands unfasten his belt while he kicks his own shoes off. "Me? You're the one with the eyes like a siren's."

I slowly lay back on the bed, watching him strip while I wiggle out of my thong to let my fingers go to my lower lips freely, and I gasp at how ready for him I am already.

"You know what sirens do to men, don't you?" I tease, but my heart flutters in my chest again when he pulls his trousers down to reveal a massive, thick cock, already stiff and immediately hardening completely as his hand wraps around it gently.

"If this is a test of my willpower," he plays along, kneeling down on the bed and putting an arm on either side of me to loom over me, "then you've already won."

He lowers himself onto me, and I melt into his kiss, letting his tongue delve into my mouth ravenously.

He pulls back from it, and I put my hand behind his neck to beg him back to me, but instead his lips dive for my neck, and I let out a silent gasp as his teeth graze the sensitive skin.

His cock is stiff and grinding against my wet cunt, hungry to delve into me, but as he starts to move it to impale me on it, I gently push him back from me, despite the protests of my body.

"Something wrong?" he asks in a husky voice as he come to a stop.

"Condom," I breathe, my hands going to my nipples to make up for the pause in stimulation.

I see his thick arm reach to the nightstand and pull a drawer open, but all I can focus on is the heat of his body. His muscular legs are brushing against my sensitive inner thighs, and I want to beg him to hurry up.

I watch him tear open the little package he withdraws and slip the thin material over his massive, bulging crown, enveloping the thick girth of the cock down to the neatly trimmed base.

"Don't keep me waiting any longer," I urge him, every tense moment of the past few months eager to melt away under him, and he obliges.

The man I met earlier this evening lowers his stiff cock to my pussy, and the tip presses against the outside. A gasp escapes me, and I realize how badly I want this.

I grip the sheets hard as he teases me, rubbing the dark crown against my needful clit. I let my head lie back on the soft sheets, and I feel his powerful hands gripping my ass, the huge cock making its way into me gently.

"You're mine, tonight," his voice growls, that deep, accented rumble sending warmth through my body and up to my face.

"Prove it," I dare him, and the next moment I let out a scream of ecstasy as he pulls me up and himself into my cunt, the fiery heat of his cock filling me like it was what I'd needed for ages and never realized.

He drapes my legs up on either side of his shoulders, broad hands on my hip and the small of my back as he starts rocking himself into me.

I can already feel the tension in my body letting loose, the man's cock sweeping it away with every gentle thrust into me. Conscious as he is of me, I feel his hands under me and realize he's in complete control, almost holding me up with his arms alone, able to move me around however he likes.

I'm so tight around him, and I try to move my hips in rhythm with his as best I can, but there's so much of the muscular figure surrounding me that I feel like a plaything in his hands as his thrusts start to get faster.

Harder.

I take silent cues from the gentle motions of his hand beneath me tells me when to twist my hips just so, and each time I heed him, the new angle works a side of me I hadn't even realized was tense, and his rhythmic breaths are punctuated by my irregular gasps of pleasure.

What am I doing? I abandoned the club, I left Natalie on her own, I-

My guilty thoughts are cut off as the man leans forward, pinning my arms down on either side of me and rutting into me furiously now.

The feeling of his shaft pumping in me at a faster and faster rhythm, the man looming over me totally controlling my every move even though I don't even know his name. Owning me for one night. Making me his.

Tension winds up in my stomach as I feel muscles contracting. My pussy is already tight around him, but my abdomen tightens further as I clench my eyes at the unstoppable wave of what's to come.

My every reflex wants to jerk away from the sensation, to just come and quickly ease myself out of it like when I touch myself on lonely nights at my apartment, but this man isn't letting me.

I'm a complete puppet to his desires, to his hunger, and I feel his breath hot on my neck as his bucking gets even harder and starts to become less and less regular.

My orgasm bursts through me like floodgates crashing open, and I let out a long, relieved gasp of pleasure and release even as I can feel the man's condom filling up inside me, the electric sensation rippling through both our bodies as he continues to ram himself into me.

I'm able to crack my eyes open through the feeling, and even through the truly overwhelming stimulation I can read on his face, there's focus, like he's pressing on and denying his own body the reflex to recoil that he's denying me.

Our bodies let themselves drop into relaxation after a few moments, and as he lowers his hot body onto me, his chest brushing against my sensitive nipples and hot breath washing over my neck, my legs tremble as our intense orgasms start to ebb, his shaft still totally submerged in me.

"Oh...my God," I manage between breaths, "you don't know how...how much I needed that."

He lifts his head, and his fingers gently guide my

chin to turn my head and look at his chiseled, smiling face.

"Believe me," he says before bringing my lips to his for a long kiss, "I can tell."

I let a long breath out, feeling utterly exhausted and defeated on the bed, but his cock is so hot inside me, and still so hard. Any motion I make makes me gasp as the sensitive skin moves around his member.

My hand goes to his face, and he lets me touch it as if I were examining a piece of art, particularly as my index finger brushes his soft, thick lips. I can feel his hand stroking my side.

The only pang of remorse I feel is when he finally draws himself out of me, getting up off the bed and stepping to the bathroom.

"I'm going to wash up," he calls over his shoulder as he steps inside, "you're welcome to stay the night."

I blink and turn my head to look at the clock.

3:00 AM.

"Fuck," I whisper to myself. *I wasn't around to close the club!*

I don't wait a second longer than the man closes the bathroom door to spring out of bed. Or try to, at least, as I almost fall to the ground on wobbly legs. But I power through it as I scramble to get my clothes on.

The club never closed. Natalie is surrounded by partiers. She's gonna quit tonight. The club is in ruins. It's actually on fire. It's already been bought by someone, there's broken glass and rubble everywhere, oh my God!

Those thoughts race through my head as I rush for the door. I pause for just a moment, casting a glance that lingers on the bathroom door where that statue of a man is running a hot shower.

I don't let myself dwell on the thought of how good it would feel to dive in with him, and I make a beeline for the door and call a cab back to the club.

A few minutes later, the driver is pulling up to the curb, and I see Natalie locking the front doors and strolling down the walkway, twirling the keychain around her finger.

Her face brightens into a cheery smile as she sees me clambering out of the taxi, flustered.

"Nothing fell to pieces while you were gone," she chimes before I can say anything, meandering over to the curb where I'm standing, the taxi still running behind me. "The partiers got drunker, they eventually wandered off, and your VIP lounge emptied out almost as soon as you were gone. We made a killing."

At this point, I'm opening and closing my mouth trying to protest something. What, exactly, I don't know. Natalie reaches me and rests her hands on her hips, smiling smugly in knowing I don't have a thing to legitimately fret about.

"So? How was it?"

I let out a defeated sigh and lean back against the cab, looking up at the sky as I cross my arms.

OWNED BY THE HITMAN

"Great. Fantastic, even." I turn my eyes to look at Natalie sidelong and add with a guilty tone, "You didn't happen to, uh, catch his name, did you?"

Natalie bursts out laughing, and I join a moment later as she playfully slaps me on the shoulder.

"Oh my *God*, Katy!"

"I know, I know, shut up!" I run a hand through my hair, embarrassment showing in the color in my cheeks even as I laugh. "But really," I start again, giving Natalie a genuinely grateful smile, "I needed a night off. Thanks, Nat."

"Just keep an eye out for him when he swings by again," she teases with a wink at me, "and get his damn number next time! Come on, I'll walk you to the cars."

As the sounds of our heels clicking on the asphalt of the parking lot echoes through the street, my smile fades before too long.

Even if Natalie can help me come to grips with the fact that I can't work around the clock, I can't deny the fact that I can't even look at this club of mine without feeling a pang in my stomach.

I don't know what the feeling is. Dread? Worry over the fact that, for all Natalie's protests, I can't do this every night? The feeling that I'm trapped keeping this place running? Yeah, probably all of the above.

Even as I watch Natalie's motorcycle pull out of the lot and I start the ignition of my own car, the vibration sending a shiver of a reminder of the night up my body, I can't help but think about how uncertain the future is. I might own a club, but this place is only scraping by month to month. The only thing keeping it up is my hard work.

The work never runs out.

And debts are due soon.

KATY

*I*t's been three months since I let myself take a night off with the suited stranger at my club. I dressed up the night after, even if I didn't want to admit I was doing it consciously, but all it earned me was a few compliments from the regulars. He didn't show.

The same thing happened the next night, and the next, and so on, until I finally stopped counting and figured he regretted something about the night.

I'm fine with it. I'm not the kind of lady who likes any more commitments than she has to take on, and right now, I have enough pre-existing commitments to worry about as it is.

The rain is pattering on the glass floor-length window of my apartment. "Floor-length window" being singular — my place isn't half as ritzy as most of the other club owners' in Brooklyn.

It has a charm of its own, though. Cozy, hard-wood floors, and a decent view of a park below from where the windows face out onto the streets of Brighton Beach. It's no dump, but it's easy to find better places to call home on this side of town.

None of them are anywhere near my price range, though.

I'm padding around the apartment barefoot with Natalie, making a mental checklist of some of the junk I have laying around the place and writing them down on the tablet in my hand.

I raise an eyebrow at a couple of old art pieces I bought a few years back, now hanging on the light cream-colored walls near the windows.

"Aw, come on, Katy, the room's gonna look like a hospital without a *few* odds and ends to make it seem lived in," Natalie protests when she sees me eyeing the pieces. "You couldn't get much for 'em, anyway."

"Right now, each of them doesn't mean much more to me than its price tag, honestly," I reply flatly.

I stroll around the house, perusing a few other odds and ends.

"Let's see...that old computer could be sold for scrap parts, probably. And these old car speakers, I don't even know why I have those laying around in the first place. Some dusty college textbooks I never got more than a few weeks' use out of, those are definitely going."

I'm selling my stuff. A lot of it. As much of it as I can live to part with, in fact. Just as I'd had to cough up for my debts three months ago, and each month after that, the time is here once again to pay my dues. My dad's old debts on top of the 'protection money' which just means they won't rough me up, add up to a lot.

And I don't have the money, I admitted to Natalie just a few hours ago over the phone. I stop taking inventory a moment to flop down on the couch — which I can also probably part with too, I decide.

Natalie is frowning at an old lamp in her hands.

"Tch, seriously Katy, you've paid your dues on time every month since this stupid debt fell into your lap. Won't they, you know, cut you a little slack? It's not like you *can't* pay, it'll just be a couple more days."

When Dad passed, I inherited more than just the Amber Room. Dad liked to gamble, and the Russian mob in Brighton Beach ran all the rackets. Turns out, Dad wasn't such a lucky guy.

"It's the mafia, Nat," I let out in an exasperated breath, "being late on payments is first on the list of things not to do."

Up until now, I've been able to scrape by. Barely.

But the debts are due soon, and I realized too late that I'm short. So here I am, pawning off my old stuff on my tablet and silently hoping that Natalie is right.

Hidden expenses rack up, running a night club.

Sure, it seems like it's just a matter of balancing the monthly bills with the income from drinks and cover charges, but maintenance fees start building up in waves. Every few months, someone breaks a barstool or a window or there's a problem with the sound system and not only do you have to shell out for that but also the DJ you hired won't work under these conditions and you have to scramble to pay another one last-minute and...

My thoughts are spinning like car tires in mud, and I clutch my head, holding back the sobs I feel welling up in my chest.

"I can't live like this," I say in a thick voice to Natalie, refusing to let myself cry in front of her. I can feel her eyes on me, though. "Hell, I don't know if I *will* live like this when the mob finds out I won't be able to make my payments."

Sitting up on the couch, I fold my legs beneath me and reach for the glass of cheap wine I have on the coffee table. My eyes wander across the room to an open box of old sports paraphernalia. A few signed baseballs, team pictures, postcards, mostly Mets stuff.

Can't sell any of that. Those belonged to Dad.

I stand up and make my way over to the box, pulling out a baseball and tossing it up and down thoughtfully.

You piece of shit, why'd you leave me to clean up this mess? You knew Mom and Steve weren't gonna be around to help me with this. You really couldn't find one of your goddamned Good Ol' Boys to help you out with money? Nobody owed you any favors, really?

Maybe I should just sell this crap.

But tears start to well up in my eyes at the thought, and I tear my eyes away from the box, pushing it under the couch so Natalie won't bring it up later.

Unfortunately for me, she proves adept at finding sour memories on her own.

"Tragic accident?" pipes up Natalie from across the room. My heart sinks as I glance over to see her poring through a stack of wrinkled old newspapers. "Wow, August 27, 2012. Why do you still have this stuff? You pack rat," she adds with a giggle.

"Uh, it's just some personal stuff," I say hastily, and step across the cluttered floor to try and take the pile of papers back. Natalie cocks her head and I can see the little cogs turning in her brain as she puts two and two together.

She puts a hand on my shoulder and gives me an apologetic look. "What is it?"

I tuck the newspapers under my arm and turn away. I knew this would come up eventually. I just didn't expect it to be now, while I have so much else going on. But when it rains, it pours, I suppose.

"I was in class when it happened. A summer class — intro to biology," I begin quietly. The memory comes trickling back into focus. I was nineteen then, just starting out in college and totally absorbed with sorority life, with studying and partying in equal doses. "A cop came into the lecture hall and interrupted the professor to ask for me."

"Oh no," breathes Natalie.

"Yeah. They drove me to the hospital and I waited in the surgical ward for hours. All three of them were there. My mom, my little brother Steven, and my dad," I say slowly, swallowing back the lump in my throat. It's still hard to think about, even after a few years. Sometimes when I close my eyes I can still remember the smell of the hospital.

After a moment I continue. "Well, my dad was driving when the brakes went out on the bridge. He swerved so he wouldn't hit the car in front of him but the car spun out and hit the railing on the left side. My mom was in the passenger seat and Steven was in the back behind her. They got the worst of it. Obviously, Dad pulled through after some stitches and a concussion. But my mom and brother... they didn't make it."

"Oh my God. I'm so sorry, Katy. I met your dad shortly before he died. He's the one who hired me, and he was a great guy. But you know better than I do, he was all business. I had no idea what kind of stuff you guys went through."

I shrug, rolling the newspapers up and out in my hands — a nervous tic I've developed. I always have to keep my hands busy with something. I know I'm strong, but I guess all that trauma has to come out some way or another.

"Yeah, Dad and I have that in common," I admit lightly.

"Hey," Natalie says with a gentle faux-punch to my arm, "you're a tough kid. And maybe I didn't know him for very long, but I can tell you without a doubt that he would be *so* proud of you."

"Thanks, Nat," I reply. But it's hard for me to believe her words, knowing how close to falling apart I am, so close to losing everything my dad worked so hard for.

She sits down on the floor cross-legged and picks up a black binder full of baseball cards and photographs. A grin spreads across her face and she looks up at me.

"This all his stuff, I imagine?" she asks.

I nod and sit down across from her. "Yep. Dad was a huge baseball fanatic. I was eight when Steven was born and I remember my dad trying so hard to get him to say "Go Mets" as his first word."

Natalie laughs. "But that's two words!"

"I know! That's what my mom said, too," I reply with a chuckle. "But his first word ended up being 'Kate,' much to my father's disappointment."

"That's adorable. You must've been his hero, Katy."

"Yeah. There was a pretty wide age gap, you know. Eight years. But he was still like my best friend in a lot of ways. We used to quote cartoons at the dinner table to annoy Mom and Dad. They could never figure out what we were talking about. I miss him a lot," I say with a sigh.

"I can't even imagine," Natalie says.

"It helps being busy all the time, you know," I reply, trying to brighten my tone.

"Well, running the club definitely keeps you on your feet."

"That's for sure," I murmur. "I just hope I can keep it afloat. I kinda feel like the club and I are both running on fumes at this point."

"Owning a business is a lot of pressure, Katy," she replies, shaking her head. "But you gotta realize that you're not alone in this, okay? We're all here for you. I know it sucks that all those guys quit when your dad died because they couldn't handle working there without him around. I get that. I can't really blame them. They were all good friends and some people just can't cope very well. Just know that they didn't leave because they wanted to abandon you, alright? And either way, you got me, Ashton, Charles, and the rest of the crew on your side. We won't let you or the club go down without a fight."

"I know. I'm lucky to have you guys around," I answer, beaming. Despite the burden on my shoulders and the dark cloud of an unpaid debt looming over my head, it really did feel good to know that my employees were in this for the long haul.

"So, weird question: is this on the list of things to sell?" Natalie asks, holding up the binder of baseball cards. I stare at it for a long moment, pondering what degree of guilt I would suffer if I were to sell my dad's beloved memorabilia.

"I don't know," I answer uncertainly.

"Because I can tell you right now, some of these cards are probably worth a pretty good amount of money at this point. Nothing too insane, of course, but it could help," she explains. "But that's only if you're okay with it. I know it's hard to let go of stuff like this sometimes. No judgment if you decide to just hold onto it."

I bite my lip and shake my head slowly. "I might have to put that on hold."

"Totally understandable. We'll put it in the "not today" pile."

I start looking through the online auction pages on my tablet, checking the competition. "Maybe I could sell my body parts on the black market," I muse aloud.

"I hear kidneys go for, like, ten thousand each or something," Natalie says, playing along.

"Oh, that's perfect. I don't need my kidneys anyway. What have they ever done for me?"

"And ten thousand is enough for, what, two months? Best idea yet."

"What about my liver? Surely I can do without that."

"Katy, you own a club. Where alcohol is served. Your liver is very important."

We both laugh and I get to my feet. "On that note, do you want any more wine? I know I could really use something to make this a little less depressing."

Natalie yawns and slides her phone screen open, squinting at the digital clock. "Aw man. Actually, I think I need to head out. I'm supposed to meet my mother for dinner, unfortunately."

"Oh, that sounds like a good time," I say from the kitchen. I hear Natalie scoff in disagreement. I open the refrigerator and pour myself another glass of wine.

"Yeah, listening to my mom list the many reasons why she's disappointed in me is always a real party," she retorts, and I can almost feel her rolling her eyes.

"Do you want a shot or something before you go, then?" I offer, only half serious.

She laughs and waves her hand dismissively. "Don't tempt me, Katy. The last thing I need is for her to accuse me of being an alcoholic, too!" She gets up and opens her arms to hug me before she plucks up her bag and sweater.

"Good luck with all this," she says to me before she leaves.

I shrug. "I got it. No big deal. I'll see you tomorrow, okay?"

"Yep. I'll be the one behind the bar."

And with that, she walks out into the hall and

gets into the elevator. I plop down on the couch again, swirling my glass of wine absentmindedly. Looking around the room at all the memories strewn about, I heave a sigh, realizing that I still don't know what the hell I'm even going to do. I start researching how much I could sell my couch for, when suddenly there's a sharp knock at the door. I glance over in confusion. It's eight o'clock at night.

Then it hits me. It's probably just Natalie. Maybe she forgot something — or perhaps she's decided she wants to take that shot, after all. I smile to myself as I cross the room to answer it.

When I turn the lock, I'm knocked back from the door as it gets shoved open, and I hear the voice of the man in the back greeting me through my sharp cry.

KATY

"Katy, darling! How good to see you again!"

The three burly Russians who muscle their way into my home are Oskar, Nic, and Konrad, the mob's collections agents assigned to me. I scramble back, wide-eyed and heart pounding as they advance into the room, Nic taking a post by the door while the other two fan out and survey the place.

Oskar is the leader of the group, and he usually does all the talking. He's a shorter guy with blonde hair and a beard, and he's as insipid to listen to as he is to look at. He's not the most muscular of the three, but he's got the sharpest tongue by far.

Nic is the quiet muscle. He's a monstrous brute of a man, all muscle and stony eyes. I've never heard him say more than a couple of words, but he doesn't need to say much that his muscles don't say for him. He has cropped dark hair and a scar across his face.

Konrad is somewhere in between the other two, and he sends chills down my spine. He's tall and lean with light brown hair and a crooked nose, and he always looks at me with an unnerving hunger in his eyes. His tendency to move suddenly and make jerking glances when he's around me all tell me he wants me, badly. He doesn't seem to like taking orders from Oskar, but I know Oskar brings him anyway because of how vulnerable he makes me feel.

"Hard to believe it's that time of the month again, isn't it?"

"That's right," I breathe, moving carefully around the coffee table, "and I'll have your money for you tomorrow before opening, just like always, you don't have to worry about me forgetting the drill."

"Of course not," Oskar chuckles, no mirth in his heavily accented voice. Konrad advances into the room, and I back away as he moves, making room for Oskar to stride in and survey the disarray of my place.

"You've done a lovely job of picking up where your father left off, Katy, always on time." He reaches a hand to me and pinches my cheeks condescendingly. "He'd be so proud! He was always the sort who knew when to do what was best for his little business."

As the blood boils under my skin and I hold back

the urge to claw his eyes out for daring to make light of the subject, Oskar flops down on the couch, kicking his feet up on the coffee table and spreading his arms out over the back of the couch.

Konrad hasn't moved since backing me up against the window. He's standing uncomfortably close to me, and I can hear his breathing. Nic hasn't moved from the door, standing there like a sentinel.

"This is just a courtesy call," Oskar drones, checking his nails idly while he makes himself comfortable. "You know, we've had a few of our boys come through the Amber Room over the months."

I know that some of the clubbers have been Russians, but in Brighton Beach, that's about a third of the clientele anyway. Not all the Russians are with the mob, but there's no way to check, either.

"Oh really?" I feign ignorance, "Can't say I've noticed. I've got a lot of guys with hot accents that pass through, and it's rude to ask all of them about their work."

Konrad likes my words a little more than I'm comfortable with, and I hear a rumble from his chest as he moves almost imperceptibly closer to me, as though he's extending his creepy aura my way. Oskar is laughing.

"Maybe so, maybe so. Come, get comfortable." The order is directed more at Konrad than me as he pats the couch cushion next to him. I feel Konrad's eager hand on the small of my back, pushing me towards the couch.

Before I can react, he takes the opportunity to put his hands around my hips and spin me around, thrusting me down on the couch next to Oskar and taking a seat on the other side of me. His hand is itching to slide around my waist, but I don't think he dares act out of turn around Oskar.

"You know, usually," Oskar starts, tilting his head and looking at me as though he were a patron flirting with me at the club, "the boys, they have nothing but good things to say about your place. Good music, not too big, classy atmosphere, and let me tell you, some of my boys, they have expensive tastes!"

I don't like where this is going.

Oskar flexes his hands, raising his eyebrows as though about to deliver bad news. "But lately, they say the crowds are a little thin, you know?"

"Really? From what I can tell, we've had outstanding retention with the regulars," I half-lie. The club has indeed had more repeat customers in the past month, but Oskar is right, the spontaneous nightly crowds haven't been out in force lately.

Konrad takes the opportunity to elbow me lightly. "Don't interrupt the boss," he grunts.

"You may be right," Oskar continues despite our interjections, "my boys, their eyes are not always so good, you know? Could be that they don't have good eyes like you."

I know I can't break the gaze he's locked me in but there's something in his eyes that makes me want to squirm as they bore into mine.

"But my thinking is that since baseball season is over, your business boom is dying down a little, no?"

I swallow and pray he doesn't notice. "You can't rely on a sports season to keep crowds all year 'round, Oskar."

"No, I am seeing this now," he smiles wickedly, and I feel my mouth grow dry as I realize I've played into his trap, "maybe this success of yours over the past few months, it was just ah, how do you say, 'riding the coattails' your father left for you in the middle of the season?"

Involuntarily, my fingers ball into a fist on the couch next to me, and I shudder as I feel Konrad put his clammy hand over it warningly.

Oskar crosses his legs and folds his hands over his knees. "But look at me, I'm being terribly presumptuous! I would never want to question your skill as a businesswoman, Miss Foss." The name is said with biting condescension, and I realize there's nothing I can say to persuade these pigs of anything. They're here for their own amusement.

"The club scene is not one you can predict so easily, and even the best of businesspeople can have a club go under, if the limelight shifts on a whim." He's looking out the window wistfully, trying to contort that sleazy face of his into a philosophical expression. It really just makes him look like he's trying to pass a kidney stone.

The next moment, Oskar stands up abruptly, leaving Konrad with me on the couch. As soon as Oskar's back is turned, I feel Konrad's hand copping a feel up my back, and goosebumps rise on my arms.

The fair-haired mobster steps around the house, perusing the items that have been taken down to be sold off. My heart sinks as I realize he's putting two-and-two together.

"But a shrewd woman like you, she puts away some money for the hard times like this, no? That would be the wise thing to do, I think. Otherwise, even a lovely woman like yourself could be pushed to give away things she doesn't want to part with."

Oskar's perceptiveness astounds me as his eyes fall on the box of Dad's baseball goods. My heart sinks in my chest, and the faintest, cruelest of smiles comes across his face as his eyes catch sight of the blanching of my face.

He bends down to pick up a signed baseball, tossing it up and down in his greasy hand as though it were just a toy.

"Hah, I used to play a little, you know?" He turns his eyes to Nic, who's been standing like a statue by the door. "Used to be a pitcher, and they told me I had a damn good arm, too. What do you think, Nic?"

Without further warning, Oskar winds up his pitching arm and sends the signed baseball full-force at Nic's stomach, and the sound of the pop the impact makes evokes a wince from even Konrad. Nic's face is utterly unfazed, but he gives an approving nod.

Oskar has heinously aggressive "short man" syndrome. Little shows of masculinity like this are all too common, I imagine, but to interrupt them in any way would be more destructive to everyone around him by a long shot. He chuckles to himself as the old ball rolls back to his feet across the floor.

"Really though, Katy, back to business," he says, making his way into the kitchen and opening my fridge to rummage around a little, finally taking out a beer and popping the top off as he helps himself to it.

"I used to own a club just like yours, Katy," he sounds suddenly friendly, stepping forward and smiling at me. I notice that Konrad's hand is still on my back, even though Oskar is looking at me evenly.

"Well, okay, not quite like yours, but close. Mine was a little more, ah...it catered to different tastes, to a different crowd." I can hear Konrad suppressing a laugh as his grin grows wider.

"And all my employees, they were the loveliest women Brighton Beach had to offer. Some of them with golden locks that spilled down their back like a golden river, some with eyes like rainy skies you could get lost in forever as they danced for you...!"

I suppress a grimace. The strip clubs around town are full of hard-working women, and I can't stand the thought of those dedicated workers being at the whim and mercy of this pig.

"Some of them were fine little things with long brown hair," he adds, his eyes narrowing at me as he reaches out to take my chin in his hand, turning me over like a piece of meat. My jaw clenches.

"I would hate for a fine business like yours to fail at paying its dues, Katy," he resumes a facade of professionalism, stepping back and peering out the window. "If you aren't able to pay the debts all the other hardworking business owners can pay responsibly, well, you know I can't guarantee the safety of your business."

I know it's a threat, and I know better than to derail his machismo. "Of course, Oskar, that won't be a problem."

"Won't it?" He casts a sidelong glare at me that is almost as terrifying as Konrad's subtle groping.

Oskar lets out a deep sigh, turning to face me with a sudden longing in his eyes that chills me to the bone.

"My girls, Katy, they were so dedicated. They often left the men who visited my little establishment wanting so much more, you know? And who am I to deny paying customers?"

He moves closer to the couch, looming over me with a deadly serious face.

"All the paying men of the city really want from such lovely women is satisfaction, Katy. They can't control their desires. And if talented women tease such men who can't control themselves, are they not to blame when such men throw money at me to help them satisfy these cravings of theirs?"

Konrad is breathing heavily next to me, and I want more than anything else to be somewhere else. Anywhere else. To just tear away from these men and flee, to Natalie's house, to the nearest train station, anywhere but here!

Oskar crouches down, and I can see the quiet hunger in his eyes. "Do you ever leave your patrons with such lingering cravings, Katy? Do you ever suppose some of them might pay to slake such a thirst?" He tilts his head to the side. "Four thousand a month, maybe?"

"More than that," Konrad rasps practically into my ear, and now he slides his cold hand up my arm and to my shoulder where it stops to play with my hair, and I hear him lick his lips even though I deny him the satisfaction of looking him in the eyes while he plays with my helplessness.

Oskar laughs with cruelty. "Ah, see? You could have your first customer, you pretty little minx. Konrad here has had such an arrangement on his mind for quite a while, you know. He'd be a fine regular for you. Maybe even Nic would like a turn with such a lovely thing as you?" He turns to the door, and Nic is only staring a cold, dead stare at us.

"But you wouldn't have to worry, dear," Oskar resumes, running a hand through my hair after brushing Konrad aside, "with someone like me watching over you, you'd be safe as you are now. Safe and secure."

The lust in his voice is palpable.

I say nothing, not because I'm restraining myself, but because I'm speechless, staring at Oskar aghast, wanting nothing more than to shove him out the window and face whatever retribution would come from Nic and Konrad afterwards.

The thug shrugs lightly, standing up as though he'd been having light conversation with me all this time. "Something to think about before tomorrow, no?"

He gives a nod to Konrad, who gives a rueful look and hesitates before withdrawing his groping hands and standing up, taking his place at Oskar's side.

"Sleep well tonight, Katy," Oskar says after finishing off the beer, tossing it into the box of baseball stuff. It lands on an autographed photo, and the frame cracks loudly. "We'll see you bright and early tomorrow. It's a big day for you, I think!"

I nod numbly. The thugs don't wait for a

response. They never wanted one: they've done what they came to do.

Nic opens the door as Oskar mutters something to him in Russian, and I can hear the three of them chattering to each other as they exit, slamming the door behind them so hard it rattles the windows.

Before I realize it's over, I'm curled up into a ball on the couch, staring at the door after them. When the sounds finally die off, a sob bursts out of me, unable to be held back any longer. I bring my sleeves up to my face and cry into them, utterly shaken by how easily they invaded my home and touched me, just barely held back by their boss's orders.

They can't do this. They can't do this. They can't threaten me like this, why are they doing this to me? Why me?!

I don't know how long I'm on the couch crying, but by the time I withdraw my sleeves, they're soaked in my tears, and my chest feels sore. I suddenly feel ashamed of myself.

What, some goons come in and try to scare you, and you're just gonna let them have the satisfaction of succeeding? My shaking hands ball into fists, and my jaw clenches as my eyes look to the box of Dad's stuff. I stand up and pad over to it, picking up the beer bottle and staring at the broken glass from the shattered frame.

Fine, I decide, *they want to play this game? I'll play.* I move back to the coffee table and pick the box of stuff up, accessing the sites where I've been posting all the items I've been trying to sell.

One by one, I start taking out Dad's old stuff and listing them online.

Natalie was right, I discover before long: some of these old relics are worth a hefty sum. If those creeps think they're going to march into my club tomorrow and use *me* as collateral, they've got another thing coming.

Of course, that's not what I want to do. What I really want is to call up Natalie, get her to round up a mob out of whatever connections she's got, track down those goons, and have their houses trashed, but my better judgement decides it's probably best not to start a one-woman war with the Russian mafia.

As I post my Dad's memories online for sale, I make my way to the medicine cabinet and take out some sleeping aids. I've got a little wine left, and I'm going to need all the help sleeping tonight I can get...even if that does mean a little self-medication is in order.

Tomorrow is going to be the longest day of the month.

KATY

I'm slow getting ready for work today.

Every tick of the clock on the wall reminds me of how harrowing my situation is. Today is the day, and I have nothing for them. I stand in front of the foggy mirror in my tiny bathroom, searching for my face amidst the condensation clouding the reflection. I rub a circle of clarity into the mirror's surface and blink sadly at myself. I look like hell.

I spent the whole night agonizing over what to do, and I'm still at a loss.

At three in the morning I was still digging through online auction sites, posting ads for every piece of decent clothing, every nonessential I own. My eyes are pink-rimmed from hours of staring at a laptop screen in the dark, and my back aches from the tense position I was perched in all night. I guess I must have fallen asleep sitting up around eight o'clock, my neck bent at a totally not-normal angle. I was certainly feeling that now, as I stretch my limbs in the shower and tried my best to feel like a regular person.

For as long as I can remember, taking a long, hot shower has been the best form of therapy for stress. After my dad died, I used to sit in the bathtub and let the steaming water pelt my cheeks until the tears stopped falling. And it is still what I turn to in times of stress — which comprises most of my waking hours these days, as it turns out.

I always thought that by this age, I would have things more figured out. Then again, I never expected to lose my whole family by the age of twenty-two, either. But life has a funny way of forcing you into places you've never been, and forcing you to become a person you never planned to become.

I blow-dry my hair and plait it into a simple braid over my left shoulder, then apply just enough makeup to make it less obvious that I haven't really slept. My phone starts buzzing on the bathroom counter and I press the stop button — my eleven AM "get up and go to work" alarm. I sigh and slip into a pair of dark jeans, black kitten heels, a scarlet off-the-shoulder tank top, and throw a black blazer on top of it all to inject some professionalism into the look. I need an outfit that is both comfortable and indicative of my position as the owner of the club.

I'm trying not to think about the fact that I may be selecting an outfit for my own appointment with the gallows. Or, more accurately, the mafia.

My mom used to always say that if you're going into a bad situation, you might as well look good getting there. It's a piece of advice that has stuck with me ever since. I swing my purse over my shoulder and take a final glance in the full-length mirror hanging on the back of my bathroom door. I *do* look pretty good, especially considering the lack of sleep and, well, everything else I've got going on at the moment. Thank God for small miracles, I suppose.

Locking the door behind me, I click-clack down the hall to the elevator and ride it down to the first floor. There's a hunched little old man in the elevator who gives me a sweet smile. I'm sure I've met him before — he's probably one of my neighbors. I try to remember his name as he checks his wristwatch and comments on the weather.

"Supposed to rain," he says quietly.

I nod politely, and he continues.

"You look very nice today. Don't forget an umbrella," he adds with a genuine wink as he stops off on the second floor before I can muster a thank you. I notice then that he's got a small bouquet of daisies tucked under his arm, and just before the elevator doors close, I see one of the doors open and a grinning, elderly woman throws her arms around him. Despite the anxiety brewing in my gut, a smile springs to my lips. Sometimes it's actually a relief to know that there are so many people leading happy lives out there. And some small, stubbornly optimistic part of me still hopes that one day I will find happiness, too.

The rain clouds are gathering in gunmetal-gray clusters overhead, threatening to spill at any moment. I hurry down the street to where my modest white sedan is parallel parked, unlock the door, and slip inside — just as the first few sprinkles of precipitation start speckling the windshield. With a heavy sigh, I start up the engine and make the trek to the Amber Room.

Upon arrival, I notice that Natalie's motorcycle is parked in back, with two helmets hanging on the handlebars. I can't help but roll my eyes fondly, wondering which girl she's romancing today. I remember when I first started coming around the club, back when my dad was still alive and he'd just hired Natalie, she clearly had a bit of a thing for me. It wore off quickly, after my dad died. She shifted straight from pick-up mode to caregiver mode, always checking in on me and being supportive however she could. Nowadays she is one of my very best friends, and there's nothing remaining of the former vibe.

I fish my umbrella out from under a pile of jackets and scarves in my backseat and step out into the light rain, leaping a few puddles as I cross the parking lot. Once inside, I am immediately greeted by Charles, whose wiry frame pops out from under a booth.

"Good morning, sunshine," he calls out with a cheery smile. I squint in confusion at the screwdriver in his hand and he promptly explains. "Oh, this metal table leg has been kind of wobbly and a couple patrons pointed it out last night, so I brought my tool kit to fix it up."

"You're a lifesaver," I reply warmly, fist-bumping him as I walk by on my way to the bar, where Natalie is wiping down the counter. She's humming to herself and clearly in her own little world. I clear my throat and set my purse down loudly on the stool beside me. Suddenly she does a double take over at me and breaks into a wide grin.

"Hey, short-stop," she greets me. Then she narrows her eyes and adds suspiciously, "You look rough. Did you sleep okay?"

Damn it. Count on Natalie to be the perceptive one. "Thanks," I say sarcastically.

"Oh no. Today's the day," she continues, catching on.

"Yep," I reply, resting my chin on my hands and giving her a what-can-ya-do shrug.

"What are you gonna do, kid?" she asks, leaning in closer.

"No idea."

Her eyebrows shoot up and she purses her lips. "Down to the wire, huh?"

I change the subject quickly — this is a topic I don't need her worrying about. It's my problem, and I'll deal with it. Natalie, Ashton, Charles — they're all innocent bystanders in this situation, and all I can do is hope that my failure doesn't put them in any danger. So instead, I say softly, "I couldn't help but notice the two helmets hanging off your bike. Wanna tell me how dinner with your *mother* went last night, Nat?"

Her cheeks went pink and she bit her lip. "Okay. Now that I can explain—"

"You didn't bring your mom to work this morning, did you?"

"I was actually being a perfect gentlewoman and giving Ashton a ride to work, thank you very much," Natalie retorted, fighting a smile. "She always takes the bus and you know how dangerous public transportation can be for a girl like that!"

"Oh, like she's really safer on a motorcycle with *you*?" I goad her teasingly.

Just then, Ashton comes around the corner with her blonde hair in a flouncy ponytail, looking very sweet and totally oblivious. Natalie gives me a pinched look, shakes her head ever so slightly, and I stifle a laugh.

"Hi, Miss Foss," Ashton says brightly.

"Hey, Ashton. And remember you can call me 'Katy,' okay?"

"Yes, ma'am — Katy," she replies.

"Alright, people. I'm going to be in the lounge working on some business stuff for a while if anyone needs me," I say, loudly enough that Charles can hear me from his place underneath the table. He extends a thumbs-up.

I give everyone a brave smile and head to the VIP room to lock myself in with my misery and ponder what the hell I'm going to do. It is noon now, and from previous months I've gathered that the mafia guys prefer to strike around this time. I suppose it's somewhat considerate of them to show up before we actually open at one o'clock. The last thing I need is for my patrons to catch the club owner in mid-shakedown. I've gotta put on a tough façade. It's hard enough just being a woman in charge, especially in such a male-dominant industry. Most of the other clubs around the area are run by paunchy older guys in sleazy business suits. I wouldn't be surprised if some of them are actually members of the mafia themselves. But me, I'm just a pawn, low on the totem pole. Financially, I'm barely holding it together. Emotionally, I'm starting to really fall apart, living in my dad's shadow and trying to keep his dream afloat.

So physically, I've got to look pretty damn put-together.

But here in the lounge, nobody can see me. So I pull my legs up underneath me on the velvety couch and open up my tablet, getting as comfortable as I can. Who knows how long I have before the thugs show up to ruin my day, and possibly my life?

Nervously, I scroll through pages of my own ads, hoping for a bite. But besides a few wishy-washy comments, there doesn't seem to be much interest in the stuff I'm selling. After all, none of it is particularly fancy. I live a very simple life, and the accoutrements of my existence are equally simplistic. But damn, I'd still hoped for at least a *few* offers.

A lock of dark hair works its way loose from my braid and dangles annoyingly between my eyes, as though to add just an extra pinch of frustration to my day. I sit up straight for a moment and try to tuck it back behind my ear. But it keeps falling free again, and so finally with a groan of irritation I yank the hair tie off the end of my braid and shake my head, sending the freshly-wavy hair tumbling in a brunette cloud around my shoulders.

"Whatever," I mutter aloud, raking a hand back through my hair and rolling my eyes. I hold up my phone to check my dim reflection in the black screen, to see my face framed with a mane of wild hair. So much for looking put together. Oh well, I think to myself, perhaps this cave woman aesthetic will strike fear into the hearts of the mafia guys.

My phone vibrates in my hand and the little ding-ding of the text tone goes off as the screen lights up with a text from Natalie.

It says: "stud on premises, I repeat, stud on the premises."

I furrow my brows in confusion for a moment, and then as the realization dawns on me, I can actually feel the blood draining from my face and my stomach flip-flops with fear.

The next moment, there's a soft knock at the VIP door and Ashton's sweet, timid voice says from the other side of it, "There's someone here to see you."

"Uh, tell them we're not open yet," I answer firmly to buy myself some time, hoping my voice isn't shaking as much as my hands are. I fumble to stuff my tablet back into my bag and untuck my legs from underneath myself. I smooth my tank top down and frantically try to restore some semblance of normalcy to my hair.

The door creaks open and Ashton pokes her head through, her blue eyes wide.

"Um, h-he's very insistent, Katy."

He? Did they only send one minion to collect my debt today? For a moment a barrage of wild thoughts rampage through my brain. Maybe if there's only one of them, they're planning to just drag me away. Maybe if there's only one of them, I can fight him off. I'm fairly strong! I can totally take down a burly, bloodthirsty mafia thug on my own! Totally reasonable!

"Katy?" she prods, looking a little scared. Regaining my composure, I get to my feet and walk over, my heart hammering in my chest, but with resolution in my steps.

I gesture for her to come inside for a moment, and I explain quietly and quickly, "Okay, Ashton. Everything is going to be just fine. I just need you to stay cool and go get Natalie and get both of you into the storage room, 'kay? Just hang out there and be very quiet. Don't come out, no matter what you hear."

I can see her shrinking in fear, her dainty hand coming up to cover her mouth. "What?"

I put my hands on both her shoulders and say emphatically, "You're okay. Just go hang out in the storage room, alright? I'll come get you when everything is over."

"Actually, that really won't be necessary," interrupts a deep voice with a light accent.

The VIP door pushes all the way open and there is a tall man standing there, wearing a navy-blue suit with a dark gray tie. My brain seems to flounder for a moment trying to place his face, as he looks vaguely familiar. Then it hits me.

The guy I slept with a few months ago.

"You may not recall me," he says, sidestepping Ashton and extending a hand to me.

I instinctively stand up straighter and move ever so slightly in front of Ashton as though to shield her somewhat. With some trepidation, I take his hand and give it a quick shake.

"I do," I reply swiftly. My heart races as I take in his suit, his accent that I couldn't properly identify before, his timing — he was a mafia guy. I should have known it all along. This is Brighton Beach, after all.

"Go to the storage room," I murmur to Ashton, without breaking eye contact with the Russian guy. As she moves to leave, he gives us both a vaguely sympathetic expression.

"I told you that won't be necessary. I am here of my own accord, and I tend to handle matters more, ah, *delicately* than some of my associates. There is no reason to hide," he explains. The look in his eyes seems genuine, and I give Ashton's hand a squeeze and nod for her to go.

She mumbles a fearful "okay" and slips out the door, shutting it behind her.

Closing me in with *him*.

He stands watching me for what feels like a very long minute, his hands pushed into his pockets and his expression unreadable. Despite his disclaimer, I am still completely on edge. I refuse to believe that it's possible for mafia guys to be "delicate." From all that I've seen, they don't have much of a particular proclivity for handling issues using anything but muscles and intimidation. And to be sure, this guy has no shortage of both. Standing in front of me, I note both his muscles, taut beneath his finely-tailored suit, and his piercing, dark blue gaze.

"Have a seat, if you like," he finally says, breaking the tension only slightly.

"Since this is my establishment and you are a guest, *sir*, I feel it's only appropriate if I offer a chair to you first," I reply sharply, before I can stop myself and edit my words. There goes my attitude. It's a reflex, and one that has gotten me in trouble many times before.

He shuffles his feet and fixes me with a hawk-like stare and I fold my arms over my chest in silent response. It's some kind of bravado stand-off. A few tense seconds pass and then, to my surprise, he steps past me to sit down on the couch. He crosses a leg wide over his lap and stretches both arms over the back of the couch, taking up as much room as possible. It's a compromise — he sits down first, but he takes the best seat.

Still, I feel a little smug as I sit in one of the silky gold-embroidered chairs, crossing my legs and setting my hands in my lap before fixing him with an expectant look.

"Today you owe a debt," he begins.

"And you've come to collect it," I respond quietly.

"Not quite," he answers, swiping a hand quickly over his mouth. "I know there is nothing *for* me to collect."

Heat rises in my cheeks. I'm caught. "Not at the present moment, no. But hopefully soon I can get the money—"

"There is another option," he interrupts. I furrow my brows at him and cross my arms over my chest as though it could slow my heart rate.

"Okay, I'm listening."

I can tell he wants to smile, and I'm not sure whether to be relieved or frightened by it. Then he leans toward me and opens those full lips to say, "Be mine."

I sit for a moment in dumbfounded silence. Then I stammer, "Wh-what?"

"For a year, I will own you."

KATY

*F*ury gathers like storm clouds in my head. I want to stand up and scream at him in indignation, tell him to go to hell. But this time, something stops me from speaking my mind. It's a sensation of resolve. It's the feeling of being backed against a wall. What can I do but listen to the parameters of his offer? It's not like I have any better alternatives off the top of my head.

"What do you mean?" I ask gravely.

He steeples his fingers and I am momentarily distracted by his big, strong hands. I wonder what kinds of things those hands have done, and in the back of my mind I can't help but remember what they felt like on my skin...

"You will be my woman for a year, servant to my whims and desires. I will not hurt you, unless you want me to," he adds. There's that smile again, not on his lips, but lurking in his deep blue eyes.

"In what capacity will I 'serve' you?" I ask, trying to temper my sardonic tone.

"Sexually," he replies simply, totally unabashed. I wonder if he's made this kind of offer before. How often does this happen? Or am I the only girl currently being offered the ultimatum of "pay up now or become an indentured sex servant?" Perhaps he's only mocking me.

"Are you serious?" I prompt.

"Absolutely."

"How can I know that those thugs aren't just going to show up later tonight and beat the hell out of me? How can I know for sure that you're not just conning me?" I ramble all at once.

He holds up a hand to silence me. "I am a man of my word."

"And you have the power to call them off?"

At that, the smile finally appears, lending some surprising warmth to his face.

"I have that power, yes."

"And when I met you before — was that just part of the job? Staking me out, doing some reconnaissance before moving in for the kill?" I continue. His smile disappears as swiftly as it came, leaving him stony-faced.

"I do not kill," he replies, his voice deep and serious, but there's something restrained in it.

Something shifts in the air and suddenly I feel goosebumps on my arms. I had only meant it as a turn of phrase, not literally. I open my mouth to say something — I don't know what — but he quickly stands up to leave.

"I will give you some time to consider my offer," he says with an air of finality.

As he opens the door, I jump up and ask him, "Wait, I don't even know your name."

He turns and looks at me hard. "Ivan."

"I-I'm Katy," I respond, as if he doesn't know.

"I'll be in touch," he says, and with that he disappears through the VIP door.

I slump down onto the couch and sit there in stunned silence for several minutes, my brain running in a thousand directions at once. Then, finally, I walk out of the lounge and up to the bar, where Natalie is standing looking rather pale.

"What the hell was that about?" she asks in a fervent whisper. "You okay, short-stop?"

I tap the bar with my nails and she quickly pours me a shot of bourbon, which I toss back immediately. Licking my lips, I reply quietly, "I don't fucking know. I'll get back to you on that. Uh, could you do me a massive favor, Nat?"

"Er, yeah. What?"

I slide my purse strap over my shoulder and turn to leave. "Watch the club tonight, huh? I-I think I need a night off. Sorry."

"Oh, yeah. Sure. You got it, boss."

Charles and Ashton both give me slightly panicked looks as I pass by, and I can't offer more than a simple, sheepish half-smile in response. But they'll be alright. My crew is shockingly self-sufficient, and they can handle themselves for a night.

Me, on the other hand...

Neglecting my umbrella, I walk to my car in the rain, hardly even cognizant of the water soaking my clothes and hair. I drive home in silence, even more confused now than I was when I left this morning.

* * *

I FEEL like I'm pushing my way through a dream as I make my way up the stairs to my apartment, turn the key to my door, and enter the place I've called home for the past few months.

My eyes pan the living room as I walk through it, but it's like my eyes are seeing everything through a fine mist, like the world is just a little bit out of focus.

Once again, that same question is haunting my every thought: why is this happening to me?

I slip my shoes off on the way in, and I set my purse down somewhere, but none of it really registers in my mind.

Why can't I just have a normal life? Why couldn't my dad's failing club have passed to me with no strings attached? I could have sold it to the business douches at the club for a tidy profit and move upstate, maybe finish college and settle down for a quiet life at a desk job somewhere.

That wasn't going to be my life, though.

Maybe I ripped a bunch of people off in a past life, I decide with a laugh as I make my way around the living room, staring at all the crap Natalie and I had dragged out last night.

What even is some of this junk? Looking around at all the possessions I had to sell, a pointedly empty feeling hits me from the pit of my stomach.

I hate having to deal with the Amber Room, but at the end of the day, it's the only asset I've got.

There are some old designer clothes strewn about in boxes, some paintings that served no better purpose than maybe a conversation starter for guests, and some old jewelry I only ever wear for work in the first place.

My job is my life.

The anger that's been burning low in the back of my mind flares up again, and I give one of the boxes of crap a sharp kick.

I don't even know what to be angry at, really. Should I hate myself for letting myself get into this position? At my dad for dumping this on me? At Ivan for suggesting that I...that he...

I can't ball my fists any tighter as I stomp into my room and slip out of my work clothes, just wanting nothing more than to be comfortable right now.

My bedroom is one of the few safe places I have left.

I flop back onto the soft mattress, spreading my tired bare limbs out on the comfortable sheets I worked so hard to keep clean.

"You will be my woman for a year, a servant to my whims and desires," I repeat Ivan's words at the ceiling, mockingly exaggerating his accent and making a face.

Who the hell does he think he is?

The voice in the back of my mind reminds me that he might be the only thing standing between me and getting pimped out by Oskar and his gang of goblins.

The back of my mind is an asshole.

I turn over and bury my face in my pillows, wishing I could make all this tension just...go away, if only for a little while.

But as I'm lying there on my stomach with the thought of Ivan hovering in my mind, my imagination can't help but drift back to that first night we spent together over three months ago.

After seeing what kind of body the guy has, not even that suit he was wearing today could keep me from remembering what's under it. Those rippling muscles, the look of absolute assuredness in his eyes that he would have total control of the bedroom for the next hour. I remember running my hands over those tattoos of his before he pressed that rock-hard body against me.

Snapping to my senses, I stop that train of thought in its tracks when I feel a familiar, warm tingling in my body, and I catch myself even as I'm starting to grind my hips into the bed. Shame rises to my cheeks.

This is the guy who just asked to own me for a year. To deprive me of my freedom to act outside his will, outside his grasp for twelve whole months.

...but how bad would that have sounded during the night we spent together?

After all, wasn't that half the fun of it, at the time? I'd shirked all responsibility, left all the stress and all the worry over the club behind me as I set foot into his bedroom. Now that I remember glimpses of it, it was a nice place, too. A lot nicer than what I have, that's for sure.

That's what you get from mob money, I guess.

That thought makes me angry. This guy is the *mafia*. He's a monster. A criminal.

But he isn't as bad as the rest of them, now, is he?

I turn over on the bed and stare angrily at the ceiling again, furious at the sensations plaguing my body. There's no way I'm going to let myself be the possession of some mobster who has access to anything he wants.

So why am I so wet?

My hand wanders its way down between my legs, and as my fingers brush my swollen lips through the fabric of the thin cloth covering them, I feel a comforting warmth through my body.

I also hear a hard *NO* come from my better judgment. This is the man who could determine whether a bunch of thugs have their way with me.

Absolutely not. No. Under no circumstances.

All those thoughts do is make my heart race faster as I'm slipping my underwear off.

A little whimper escapes me as I part my lips and gently start to massage my clit. There's more tension bound up in me than I realize, just like the last time I was with him. With Ivan. How did I not even get his name during the whole time we spent together?

My clit is reluctant to warm up to my touch, it's been so long, but compulsion makes me keep massaging the sensitive skin as my legs move slowly up and down the sheets, relishing in the feel of the fabric against my inner thighs.

My fingers are moving a little faster as I get wetter, and then the night I'd buried under all the stress of work starts to come back to me. How strong Ivan was, how I had wanted to wrap myself around him and never let go.

He was just some gorgeous stranger, and I let him fuck me. I might not be able to imitate how his massive crown felt diving inside me, but my hips rocked up into my touch as I remember the way he felt grinding against me, holding me so lovingly even though it was a one-night stand.

He used me, I think to myself as I feel my fingers wetten as they touch my desperate, needy cunt. My whole body has been wishing for that release again, I realize.

The thought makes my heart flutter. The body I've been wanting to press up against me, to hold me tight and hold me up with an inescapable grip while he fucks me has been that of a mobster this whole time. A hardened criminal.

I let out a soft moan, not sure where the transition from idly touching myself to torturing my clit happened, but now I'm squirming on the bed sheets, my fingers covered in my own wetness, and my heart is racing.

He wants me. After all those months, he thought of me and wants me in his bed, in his hands, and around his cock again.

Would it really feel so bad, a year under his ownership?

KATY

*M*y muscles tense and my toes clench as my mouth is forced open by the overwhelming cresting of the orgasm that follows that scandalous thought, and in a liberating moment of ecstasy, I let out a long, breathy cry of release as I feel my whole body electrified by the thought of Ivan looming over me again.

I keep moving my fingers and come again and again as my body writhes in a mixture of pleasure and shame at the thought of him, of his impossibly strong body and those dark blue eyes holding my gaze as long as he wanted.

Finally, my clit is almost too sensitive to touch, and I withdraw my hand, clenching my legs together as my body shakes and I turn onto my side to curl up as the sensations subside.

It's a few moments before I can let my hand return to my pussy, slowly and gently nursing it through the orgasm's subsiding.

My eyes crack open, and I look down at the mess I've made of myself.

Then my mouth starts to curl into a smile, and I bite my lip and turn my head into the pillows in disbelief at the silliness of the thoughts I just used to get myself off.

"You're a mess, Katy," I half-giggle at myself, wallowing in the enormous feeling of relaxation that pins me to the bed, "a perverted mess."

A few minutes later, I'm in the shower, steam pouring over the top of the clear sliding doors as I lean against the cool walls, letting my hair get soaked. I might have gotten myself off, but I'm still slick between my lips. I can't stop thinking about how great it would have felt to have joined Ivan in the shower that night.

As I start to wash the worries and pleasure of the day off my body, I can't help but wonder what actually might have been different now if I'd stayed the night with him. Would I have found out who he is? What he does? Would any of this debt issue have come up again?

Would I have liked him?

Hot water runs down my body, and that thought lingers in my mind for a while. He seemed alright that night we spent together. I never would have known a thing was amiss if he hadn't strolled into my club and announced that he's a mobster, here to do mobster things at my mobster-owned club.

I put my forehead against the wall, hugging myself while breathing the hot air around me. Maybe my body's impulses aren't entirely wrong about Ivan's offer.

I know I want this. I know myself well enough not to fool myself in that regard. But is this really the best thing for the club?

It would totally free me of my debt. I'd never have to worry about the mob breathing down my neck ever again. I'd be able to use that spare $4,000 a month for anything. Savings, maybe a new expansion, raises for all the staff of course, a decent place to live. Just the thought of all that makes me almost giddy, almost ready to forget what I'd have to do for that kind of freedom.

Almost.

What if he doesn't hold up his end of the bargain? What if he decides I'm not good enough after a few months and sticks me back to square one? What if he's not even being honest in the first place and this is just some ploy to humiliate me?

No. I can't do this.

I nod to myself, the useless gesture a silent resolution to myself. I don't want anyone else dangling charity over my head. If I'm going to weather this storm, I'll do it on my own or not at all.

It isn't worth the risk to put my life in the hands of some mobster who just wants a piece of meat to fuck for a year and toss aside. That's how criminals work, after all. None of them can be trusted. They put Dad and me in this situation in the first place, and they'll just put me right back in it when they've had their fun.

I finish washing up and turn the water off, stepping out onto the tile of the bathroom and wrapping a towel around my body. I wipe some of the condensation off the mirror and stare at my reflection.

I'm going to face whatever comes at me tomorrow, one way or the other.

* * *

THE SKY IS OVERCAST YET AGAIN as I drive to work today. I'm wracking my brain for the proper words to say, unsure how exactly to explain to Ivan that I have to decline his offer. Not that it isn't a tempting option, at least on some level I'm refusing to entertain at the moment, but my father's influence is powerful over me. I know he would want me to say no. Of course. And any woman in her right mind *would* object to her being treated like a sex slave for a year, wouldn't she? Seems pretty common-sense.

But then again, it's not every woman who ends

up in this kind of predicament to begin with. Who's to say I'm not making a huge mistake in turning down my one chance at eventual freedom from these mafia thugs? It does sound wonderful — the prospect of being able to live my life without the shadow of the mafia hovering over me and shading everything I do, every choice I make. I could finally do the things I want to do with my money. I could fix up the club a little more, add some of my own touches. I could finally give Natalie the raise she deserves. Hell, I could finally put away some money to travel, see the world like I've always wanted to.

No, I tell myself firmly, *it's not that simple*. After all, despite his claims to the contrary, I am pretty damn certain that Ivan is a dangerous, dangerous guy. Probably not the type of man I want to be chained to for a year. His "whims and desires" might actually include some messed-up stuff that I should want no part of.

So here I am with my dilemma. How does one politely tell a Russian mobster no?

As I'm pondering all the miniscule variations of "thanks, but no thanks" I pull my car into the parking lot and cross the pavement to the front door of the club. Once again, the motorcycle has two helmets dangling from it and a smirk crosses my face. Are Natalie and Ashton just carpooling (bike-pooling?) or is there something else going on I need to address? I suppose that since I'm technically their boss, I might have to lay down some ground rules about dating your coworkers or something.

But when I get inside and settle into a seat at the bar, it turns out that I'm on the receiving end of an interrogation, rather than the opposite.

Natalie and Ashton are both leaning on the other side of the bar, nursing coffees and staring at me with gleeful expressions, looking very mischievous. And to think, Ashton was such a sweet, innocent girl when she first started here. I make a mental note to goad Natalie later about being a bad influence. At the moment, I am eyeing the pair of them suspiciously, waiting for the barrage of questions to begin.

Natalie starts, of course. "So what the hell is going on with that Russian guy?"

"He's cute," Ashton adds, looking a little bashful for admitting it. I can't help but clock the slightly doleful look in Natalie's eyes for a moment.

"I guess he's kinda hot in a scary way. If you're into that," Natalie tacks on, trying her best to look nonchalant about it. "But for real, what's happening, Katy?"

"Oh, nothing," I answer quickly. Both girls open their mouths to retort, but I continue before they get the chance. "Seriously. Nothing you two need to worry about. It's fine. I'm taking care of it. It's *fine*."

"Taking care of it? That sounds bad," Ashton comments, her sweet face scrunching up.

"Taking care of what, exactly?" Natalie interjects, waggling her eyebrows suggestively.

"He's not gonna hurt you, is he?" Ashton asks, wide-eyed.

"Is he gonna be hanging around a lot?"

"Are you sure you know what you're doing? He looked real serious."

"You know you can tell me anything, right?"

I rub at my temples in frustration. I should have known this game of twenty questions was inevitable, with these two around.

"OKAY," I interrupt, holding my hands in the time-out gesture. "Well, he might be coming back today so I'm gonna need you guys to play it cool, alright? Please? Just act *normal*," I plead with them.

"He's coming back?"

"Why?"

Both of these questions hit me at the exact same time and I sigh heavily.

"Right, see this whole 'questionnaire' thing you're doing right now? Yeah. Don't do that when — *if* — he comes by today," I tell them solidly as I get up to leave the bar.

Just then there's a loud bang from down the hallway to the front door. Ashton gasps.

"Probably just Charles," I say quickly.

"He said he'd be late today," Natalie replies, looking bewildered.

A wicked male voice calls out mockingly, "Kaaaatyyyyy!"

My stomach lurches as I recognize Oskar's voice. Immediately I turn on my heel and hiss at Natalie and Ashton, "Get behind the bar. Stay down and do not make a sound, hear me?"

Ashton whimpers in an undertone, "What's going on?"

"Just hide!" I whisper emphatically, pointing behind the bar. Natalie nods and dutifully puts an arm around Ashton's shoulders to force the both of them back down behind the counter, just as a chorus of rancorous laughter echoes down the hallway.

I turn back around and walk quickly to the middle of the dimly-lit dance floor, crossing my arms over my chest and trying to look tough. I should have known not to trust Ivan. He told me that the thugs weren't coming, that he had the power to call them off. I know now that he must have lied to me — and I am suddenly relieved that I didn't take his offer. I am so furious that the anger bubbling in my stomach almost overpowers the fear I'm feeling at the moment.

The three mafia guys come skulking around the corner, two of them wearing hateful, sadistic grins, while the quiet one Nic simply stares with those cold, dead eyes. I wonder if he even feels anything at all. Then I wonder what I'm going to feel in a moment...

What if they kill me?

I close my eyes for a brief second and hope desperately that at least they might spare my coworkers. Nat and Ashton are totally innocent of all this. They deserve to live.

"What are you up to, Katy?" snarls Oskar, a crude smile on his face.

"Got anything for us?" adds Konrad. He extends his hand and makes a motion like he's rubbing coins together between his forefinger and thumb. "It's collection day."

"I told you boys I would have your money," I say, willing my voice not to shake.

"Uh huh. And where is it, sweetheart?" Oskar growls, taking a few slow strides toward me. He snaps his fingers a few times with an expectant look on his face.

I can't find the words. I have no idea what to tell him. Part of me wants to lie, to tell him I'll have the money tonight, tomorrow, sometime in the future. Maybe I can run away, go to the police or something. But I know the mafia would only find me, and they certainly would never forget. They specialize in holding grudges and delivering harsh punishments.

A small, shrill voice in the back of my mind urges me to drop to my knees and beg for my life, offer them anything, everything I have. But I know I'm too strong for that, too stubborn.

"Still waiting, bitch," Konrad barks. He walks

over to the booth Charles fixed just yesterday and plucks up the little glass votive off the table. He throws it as hard as he can on the hardwood floor and it shatters into little pieces. There is an almost inaudible gasp from behind me and my heart races, hoping that the thugs didn't hear it. *Be quiet!*

"Nic, what do we do when someone is late on their payment, huh?" Oskar says.

The hulking henchman pounds a fist into his palm and grumbles in a tone that sounds almost bored, "We charge interest."

"And if they can't pay interest… what do we do then?"

"Find an alternative method of payment," Konrad breaks in, shattering a second votive.

"For example, if you don't have cash, sometimes we'll take an equitable amount of flesh or blood instead. And let me tell you, *sooka*, the exchange rate is not so good," Oskar hisses, cracking his knuckles as he approaches me. I wince as Konrad picks up a chair and throws it across the room, sending it clattering across the dance floor and smashing against a wall.

"What do you want?" I ask, holding my head high.

Oskar cackles and puts his hands on his hips, eyeing me up and down. "Well, this debt is quite a sticky one. I think we might have to split the payment between both flesh *and* blood, wouldn't you agree, Konrad?"

"I'll take the flesh if you want to stake a claim on the blood, Nicolas!" Konrad calls out over his shoulder. Nic nods and starts lumbering toward me, arms poised at his sides and his muscles rippling with every heavy step. I feel my throat close up with terror.

"And what do I get?" Oskar says, rubbing his jaw thoughtfully. "Ahh yes, I get the pleasure of watching and the satisfaction of another business transaction carried out successfully. What more can a man ask for these days?"

He steps up to me and I freeze up as he lifts a hand to gently caress my cheek. Then he pats it a couple times and says, "Nicolas, Konrad, come."

The henchmen rush to my side and each grab one of my arms, wresting them behind my back as Oskar continues to survey me with beady, mean eyes. He steps back a few feet and clucks his tongue as though weighing his options. Then he claps his hands together.

"Okay, boys. You can have your playtime with Miss Foss. Then it's back to business."

"No," I murmur under my breath.

"Oh *yes*," Konrad purrs darkly, his breath hot and rancid on my neck. I shiver and try to jerk away from him but he only tightens his vice grip on my arm and yanks me closer. Nic stands utterly still and expressionless, stoic as always.

I gasp at the sensation of a long-fingered hand clutching my ass, sliding down the slope of my thigh and between them, his fingers rubbing at my crotch outside my jeans. I cry out in disgust and clamp my legs together more tightly, trying to fling my head back to hit Konrad. But he dodges the move easily, bringing his hand up around my neck.

"You little bitch," he rasps, laughing. "You don't have the money, and you don't want to honor our deal? You can't get out of this. You have to pay."

"I refuse to pay with my dignity," I manage to choke out. I kick backward and strike Konrad in the shin. He lets out a bellow of anguish and twists my arm, causing me to wince, tears forming in my eyes.

"You've got none of that left," he replies.

As his fingers curl around my throat, Oskar interrupts.

"Well, if our client doesn't want to play nice then we will simply have to skip to the next portion of our transaction. Nic, do your work."

I struggle as hard as I can trying to break free, my body tensing up in anticipation of the pain I'm about to endure. Nic squares up and winds his arm back to pummel me in the stomach. As he lands the first blow, I cry out in agony and buckle inward, my chest heaving as I try to suck air into my shocked lungs.

He pulls back to hit me again, with Konrad

twisting my arms more tightly behind my back, bruising my flesh and laughing low and evil in my ear. I fold in on myself, wondering if I might actually die here, right now, in the middle of my father's club.

"Don't you *dare*."

The words come from a deep voice across the room, a new voice. We all look over in surprise to see Ivan standing there, a big black gun raised and pointed in our direction. My stomach drops, as I have no idea whether he's there to save me or to finish me off.

He is wearing all black, his pressed button-up shirt half-tucked, his jacket and shoes obviously more expensive than my rent. There's dark stubble shadowing his jaw and his thick brows are furrowed in anger. His full lips are set in a hard line and I can see his finger positioned on the trigger of his gun.

"Make one more move and all three of you will be dead before you can even harm a hair on her head."

With one desperate, pleading look toward Oskar, Konrad releases me, shoving me away. Nic raises his massive arms over his head in surrender and backs off a few feet. I stumble and fall to my knees, pain radiating up and down my legs.

There's a shriek of panic from behind the bar — presumably Ashton has just seen the gun.

In the next second, there is a scramble of rapid movements, as Konrad lunges for the bar. I look over my shoulder to see Natalie and Ashton hop up from their hiding place, looking totally pale and terrified.

"Run!" I scream at them as Konrad rushes around toward the other side of the counter. Both girls let out strangled cries of fear and start to bolt, Nic and Konrad both turn to run at them, and out of the corner of my eye I see Oskar reach for something at his hip.

But amidst the chaos we all hear the dreadful click of Ivan cocking his weapon.

"Everybody stay still and shut up!" Ivan commands. And to my surprise, everyone obliges completely. With his gun fixed on Oskar, he takes several steps forward, never taking his eyes off of me.

"Set that gun on the floor," Ivan adds.

There's a pause. And then with a scathing look, Oskar draws the gun, raising his arms out as he slowly bends to the ground. I hold my breath, watching him dutifully lay the weapon down and stand back up.

"Now, all three of you pieces of shit need to leave quietly."

Once again, there is a moment of hesitation. And then the three thugs resign themselves and make their slow, hateful procession across the room toward the exit. Ivan follows them with his steely gaze until they pass him, and then he looks down at me with an expression of mingled apology and horror.

He opens his mouth to say something, but before he gets the chance, Nic charges at him from behind, tackling him to the ground, with Konrad following quickly after. In that instant, I see Oskar bolting back toward me — and realize that he is running to collect his gun. Without even thinking, I jump to my feet, ignoring the pangs of agony coming from my legs and stomach. I take a few quick, long strides and kick the gun across the floor so that it slides underneath one of the couches lining the wall. Then I spin around and spread out my aching arms in an instinctual position of protection, knowing that Natalie and Ashton are somewhere behind me.

I look up to see Ivan wrest one arm free and strike Nic hard across the back of the head with the gun. The big guy yelps in pain and falls to the floor, clutching his head. Konrad is attempting to muscle the gun out of Ivan's hand, but Ivan is too quick for him and deftly slips his other arm around Konrad's neck. With the asshole locked in a chokehold, he presses the gun to Konrad's temple, causing the thug to stop squirming and gulp hard.

Oskar is running toward the couch, desperate to get his gun. But Ivan clears his throat loudly and calls out, "Leave it, swine!"

Oskar spins around and glares at him — and then

ALEXIS ABBOTT

notices that his two henchmen are out of commission, leaving him alone to defend himself.

"One wrong step and your friend is dead."

"Kill him, I don't care," replies Oskar, but his face betrays his true feelings.

"And you'll have to explain to your boss why your team is one man short. I know you don't want to deal with that, now, do you?" Ivan counters confidently. "Besides, with just two of you left, what do you really think your chances are of getting out of this room alive?"

"We're just doing our jobs," Oskar replies plaintively.

"I called you off. This is my job now. Leave and do not come back here. If I see your ugly face in this club again I will beat you until even your own mother will not recognize you. Tell your *matushka* I said hello, by the way," Ivan adds with a cruel grin. Oskar goes pale.

"You'll regret this," Oskar snarls as he finally leaves, snapping his fingers so that Nic gingerly gets to his feet to follow. With a final tap of the gun barrel to Konrad's forehead, Ivan releases him, this time focusing the gun on the three thugs until they skulk out of sight. He doesn't move until we all hear the door open and slam shut again.

Then Ivan returns his gun to its holster and crosses the room to give me his hand. In a daze, I take it, staring wide-eyed and shocked at Ivan.

"Come. I will take you home," he says quietly but firmly. I know there is no chance of declining this particular offer.

As he leads me away, I manage to call back to Natalie, "Close up. Go home. Club is closed tonight. I will call you later."

Natalie and Ashton both whimper faint sounds of assent as Ivan half-carries me out the door and into the rain.

KATY

*M*y head is resting against the cool glass window of Ivan's car. It's a brand-new black Mercedes with a spacious interior, but I can hardly pay attention to the luxurious ride I'm being taken on with everything that's racing through my head.

I stare numbly out the window as Ivan drives. Raindrops are pattering against it, marring the view of the rainy Brighton Beach that passes by outside. We drive by the red brick shops and apartments along Neptune Avenue, and my eyes try to catch a few of the pedestrians ambling by.

It hits me as odd that the things that are happening to me are happening right under their noses. I wonder how many of them worry about or even notice the crime that riddles their own city, but more than that, I find myself kind of wishing I were in their shoes instead of mine.

Ivan must not want to try to talk to me right now, because he doesn't say anything as long as I keep my eyes steadily focused outside. A few times, my mind wanders to him, wondering what could be going on in that mind of his.

An actual fight, in my club. People got hurt, and someone very well could have died if anything had gone awry during Ivan's stunt. Not once did I ever think I'd have to deal with a gun being pulled in the Amber Room, yet here we are now.

What did I do wrong?

What would Dad think?

I tear my eyes away from the window and rub my temples. I can't let myself brood on that anymore. I'm over that threshold. Dad is the one who's responsible for my being here in the first place, isn't he? Maybe what he would think in a time like this isn't the best thing to go by.

I gave Ivan my address when we first got into the car, and now we're pulling up into the parking lot. Before I know it, he's silently gotten out, come around to the passenger's door, and started to help me out delicately.

"Careful there," he warns as I shakily stand to my feet. I didn't realize how wobbly my knees would be in the aftermath of the adrenaline rush, but I would have collapsed if he weren't helping me up. I feel a weight on my shoulders and turn my eyes to see a heavy, oversized jacket being draped over me.

Even as it warms me, I wince at the pain in my torso. I know the brutes were trying not to leave a mark on me so people wouldn't ask questions, but I know I'll have one on my stomach by morning. I feel my wrists, and they're raw too. I shudder at the thought of what might have happened if they'd been left to get carried away on their own.

I ignore the puzzled look we get from one of my neighbors passing by as Ivan helps me up the stairs and I try to unlock the door with a shaking hand. My face burns bright red when a metallic click tells me I missed the keyhole. My hands are shaking too badly.

"Damnit," I swear under my breath while vainly scratching at the keyhole before a warmth envelops my hand — Ivan has reached his out to steady mine. "Thanks," I murmur a moment before the lock clicks open and we step inside.

My apartment isn't much of a comfort right now. As soon as we walk in, I'm greeted by the sights of all the half-packaged goods I'd been trying to sell, and I'm hit by the memory of that frantic night and the morning after. My grimace deepens when I realize all of that was just in the past twenty-four hours. It feels like it's been a full week.

Ivan quietly helps me inside, his powerful muscles steering me to the empty couch easily. He's careful to ease me down slowly, and I can feel the muscles in my abdomen protest at the change, already starting to feel sore.

I resist gently as I feel him try to put me on my back, but he gives me a concerned look. "Don't try to sit up," he says in a soft voice, "I know you'll want to keep awake, but you need rest after an episode like that."

"I'm fine," I protest, pushing his hand away as I suddenly feel indignant at being treated like a patient in my own house. My face does a sorry job of hiding the pain, though.

"You've never taken a blow in your life," he answers, but there's no mockery in his tone. His eyes give me a steady, firm gaze, though. Reluctantly, I concede and lay back on the soft couch.

He takes my forearm in his hands, narrowing his eyes at the marks that are starting to show themselves. "Hm."

"What?" I ask, lifting my head a little as he gets up and heads further into the apartment. A moment later, he spots the bathroom and disappears inside.

I let my head plop back down onto the cushion, wondering at the different ways things could go from here. *So he saves me from his own goons...for what? Does he want me as his little hostage, here in my own home? I'm not that badly injured, if he thinks I'm about to roll over and let him march in on my business. Or maybe he really did just think they'd go too far, push a 'client' beyond her limits.*

None of the options put a good taste in my mouth, but I'm surprised to see him emerge from the bathroom a few moments later with some bandages, cotton, peroxide, and ointment from my medicine cabinet.

"What are you—?"

"Just relax," he insists, sitting down next to me and taking my wrist in his lap. He turns it over for a moment with a frown, looking at the bruising and scratches before dabbing a cotton ball with peroxide and dabbing the cuts gently.

I wince at the pain, but my eyes are watching his face incredulously. *Is this guy for real?*

"I won't try to apologize for scum like those three," he says. "They are the types that take pleasure in tormenting anyone they can get their greasy hands around. Not the kind of men I consider part of my business."

"You all seemed to be on the same page before today," I point out, but he doesn't give a response. He's applying ointment to my wrists now and wrapping bandage around them.

He reaches over and touches my sore spot, but even his painstakingly gentle touch makes me wince. He frowns, a low rumble coming from his chest. "The beasts meant to do a real number on you," he remarks ruefully. "I don't like to think of what might have happened if I hadn't made it any sooner. I didn't see any aspirin in the bathroom," he adds, looking back up to me.

"Kitchen," I say with a gesture in that direction, and he nods.

As he moves that way, his gaze drifts across the boxes scattered about the room, and my heart sinks as I anticipate the inevitable question.

"What's with the packing? Were you planning to move before today?"

"No, nothing like that," I stammer out, but in hindsight, I think that might have been a decent idea. "I was just...selling a few of my things, getting them ready to ship quickly."

Silence in response.

"Look," I start again, finding it easier to speak while he's out of the room just now, "Ivan, I...I don't know what they would have done if you hadn't shown up, you're right. Thank you. You might have saved my life today. Or saved me from something else, I don't want to think about..." I trail off, letting silence hang awkwardly between us again.

I don't have to see his face to know he's already put two and two together to figure out I can't make the $4,000 anymore. I just know he's going to bring his offer up again, so I scramble to say something to divert his attention when something that had been nagging at the back of my mind hits me.

"Ivan, you said you don't kill."

The bustling in the kitchen stops. "Yes."

I bite my lip and look at my carefully arranged bandages before continuing. "The way you moved in there, I've never seen anything like it. You moved like you weren't afraid to face anything they were going to throw at you," I breathe, surprised at my own outpour, but the more I think about it, the more astonishing Ivan's actions were, I realize. "You fought them like you were ready to kill. You knew what you were doing."

Ivan strides back into the room with a stony expression, and I immediately regret broaching the subject. He sets a glass of water and three white aspirin tablets on the table next to me, with a nod for me to take them.

As I do, I notice he's avoiding my gaze, but his expression is no softer.

"I said I do not kill, Katy," he says quietly, and then his eyes look up to meet mine with a chilling coldness. "What I do is business. Only business. What those three devils would have done to you, that would have been 'killing.' You had this whole ordeal dumped into your lap against your will, and you know nothing of it beyond what you are told. You're outside our business, in the grand scheme of things."

My eyes are wide as I watch him rise and move to the window, peering out at the darkening street below.

"I am not a brute, killing whatever comes into my path. But you're right. I'm not called on to handle trivial business. We Russians, we take breaches of professionalism very seriously. Those who act against us from within are no better than rats."

He turns to face me, but I can already read the words in his face. "They call on me to deal with the rats. The kind of scum who were trying to force you into something against your will."

A hit man.

My throat goes cold. I'm standing before a man who's taken the lives of others. A paid assassin.

"The men today, one of them has a powerful relative, so I had to hold back." He looks up at me now, meeting my eyes with a surprisingly gentle gaze. "I'm truly sorry to have to put you through the fear of knowing they still live."

I shake my head as though I'm saying 'no thank-you' to another helping of food — I've never exactly had someone apologize to me for not killing someone.

"Ivan," I start, but I trail off, unable to process this news. Then an even harder realization nearly makes me dizzy: I had a one-night stand with a hit man.

"You don't have to say anything," Ivan says, holding a hand up and stepping closer to me. I recoil, and he pauses, a sad look in his eyes. "I understand this is a lot to take in. Too much for even a woman as brave as yourself." He offers a smile, almost laughing. "Judging by the fact that you were ready to walk into the club and say 'no' to those three with nothing but your bartender backing you up, you've got more courage than the three of them put together."

Without another word, he reaches over me and pulls down the huge blanket I have folded on the back of the couch. He drapes it over me, and I feel his hands poking at my sides.

He's tucking me in!

"You need rest," he says with finality, those stormy blue eyes looking at me with a calming authority I can't explain. "We can talk more once you've let some of this excitement settle. In the meantime—" he stops himself, glancing around the apartment. "Never mind. For now, you've earned some rest, Katy."

He runs his fingers through my hair, and I find myself smiling despite myself. I force the smile away when I catch it, but I think he notices. He stands up with a wink and heads to the kitchen again, and I let out a deep sigh of relief, letting myself stare at the ceiling and trying to relax as many of my muscles as I can.

A hit man just saved my life. The man who was asking me to be his just yesterday. He nearly killed Oskar and the gang. Hell, he practically had to hold himself back from doing just that. And now he's...he's acting like a nurse?

I turn my eyes down to the bandages around my wrists. They're perfect. Not too tight, just snug and neat, and the ointment under them makes my skin feel cool and soothed, even though I know it'll sting when I wake up.

Wake up. It suddenly hits me how tired I am. This isn't just an exhaustion, though, I feel somehow safe around Ivan.

Why do I feel okay dozing off under this hit man's care?

Because he's still the same gorgeous guy you went home with three months ago, and on top of that, he may say he's a killer, but he's practically a teddy bear around me, I remind myself.

I can't quite tell what Ivan is doing in the kitchen, but I can hear bustling. It's reassuring. Even if Oskar and his goons were to try to come back, Ivan is there.

And after all, he didn't have to come for me today. I don't know how much of what the Russians shouted at each other was true, but somehow, I doubt the mob would have suffered too much if I'd been left to fend for myself at the three's mercy.

Sleep is overwhelming me, fast, and I want nothing more than to just let it. But one thought lingers in my mind while I'm dozing off:

Maybe...maybe it wouldn't be so bad, being Ivan's for a while.

* * *

A GENTLE PRODDING at my side and the warming
aroma of chicken wakes me up. I clench my eyes as
the soreness of my chest hits me next, but they
flutter open at the sound of a deep voice whispering
over me.

"Katy? No no, careful, don't try to turn yourself
yet."

Ivan's warm, smiling face comes into focus,
adjusting a pillow that's been mysteriously slipped
under my head.

"Ivan?" I've had one of those naps that leaves you
more disoriented than anything else, and for a
moment, fear swarms me as I remember the events
of the day. The next instant, remembering that Ivan
has been here the whole time dulls the edge somehow, and despite his protest, I try to pull myself
somewhat upright. "What are you...?"

Getting a better look at him, I almost can't
believe my eyes.

Ivan has shed his jacket and rolled up his sleeves,
revealing thick, muscled forearms, and more impor-
tantly, the powerful hands at the ends of them are
holding a large bowl of steaming, delicious-smelling
soup. The only thing missing for a perfect hallmark
moment would be if he was wearing my apron. Still,
I have to put a hand to my mouth to keep my jaw
from dropping at the sight.

"I hope you don't mind," he says with a sheepish smile, setting the soup and a napkin down on the coffee table. "I was looking for something to warm you up when you woke, but I came across some ingredients for something a little close to home. It's just chicken soup, but the way my mother used to make it." His smile splits into a genuine grin. "You keep a good stock of spices, so I couldn't help myself. It's been awhile since I've had a chance to make it. Kind of a comfort food."

I'm just stupefied for a few moments, and I pull the blanket a little higher up to my neck. A smile is tugging at my lips. I haven't smelled the aroma of home-cooked food in a long time. Running a club has meant a lot of microwave meals.

A few moments later, the two of us are sitting at opposite ends of the coffee table.

"Ivan, this is incredible," I say between spoonfuls of the broth, and I mean it. The soup warms my whole chest, relieving the soreness in my stomach in a subtle, reassuring way. "I don't know what to say. I mean, thank you!" My eyes meet his a moment, and there's an affectionate glint in his.

"It's not necessary," he says after a mouthful, setting his bowl down. "Katy, I'm sorry for every-thing this has put you through. Business is business, you understand."

"No, I do," I say hurriedly, biting my lip before

proceeding. "There's been something on my mind, and I think this is as good a time as any."

Ivan tilts his head, and I hold the warm soup close to my chest, heating the cocoon of blanket I'm wrapped in. I stare at the floor for a long while before looking into his eyes, resolution now firmer than ever, and a small smile spreads across my lips.

"I'll take your offer."

KATY

*I*t's New Year's Eve, and I still haven't told anyone about the deal.

I hold the ladder steady for Natalie as she works on the light fixtures for the big night. New Year's is always a booming event for any club, anywhere. In Brighton Beach, though, it's all the more important that everything go off without a hitch. People come from all over to start the New Year with a bang, and the Amber Room is not going to miss out on those crowds.

Especially since I've got the money to make that happen now.

To my surprise, that's been the biggest change in my life since agreeing to be Ivan's for a year. Even when I first accepted his deal, I knew the dizzying high I got from the outpour of affection wouldn't last. Later that very night, I started to worry about whether he'd change for the worse as soon as it started, but so far it's felt like, well, having a boyfriend.

He started by telling me that we were going to stop selling my stuff, and that alone took a huge weight off my shoulders. We put all of my possessions back into place, and he even helped me reorganize some of the house, which was long overdue. He hasn't even told me to move in with him, which I thought would happen right off the bat.

Instead, I've found myself with breathing room to get the club back on its feet with the spare money I have.

And I'm not wasting any time putting it to use.

"Okay Natalie, 2016. Is that motorcycle ride gonna happen for me now, or what?" Ashton chimes from across the room while she moves around the walls, changing bulbs on the floodlights. She's been trying to get Natalie to let her ride her bike since getting hired.

"What's that? Can't hear you, the lights are a little loud up here," she calls back, half-hidden in the hanging lights.

On a regular day, the ceiling looks like a starry sky, a canvas of hanging lights that make the little club seem like a ballroom. For tonight, Natalie's brought out the heavy artillery: amber lights in ornate patterns around the whole room, almost doubling the brightness of the room, set to light up at the stroke of midnight. Natalie used to work on theater sets, so she volunteered to handle the "stage-setting" for tonight.

"Tch," Ashton clicks, "you never let me have any fun."

"Do too. I let you help me wax it last time."

"That wasn't as fun as you said it would be."

"See?" Natalie winks down at me, "She doesn't even appreciate my heartfelt generosity."

I roll my eyes. "Anyway, are you sure this stuff is safe? It's been a good couple of months, but I don't think a fire inspector having an aneurism in the building would do much to keep it that way." All I've told the staff is that the payments have been worked out. They got the message not to press further.

"I mean," Natalie puts a hand on her hip, tilting her head to the side, "the chances of something happening on one night are, like, pretty slim, you know? And besides, if something does go up in flames, we can use Charlie as a wet blanket, right Charlie?"

The bouncer in the corner doesn't look up from his phone, but grunts noncommittally. He's been on dating websites all morning.

"What'd I tell ya?" Natalie grins back at me, climbing down from the ladder and scooting it over a few feet to start working on another section of the ceiling. "Anyway, everyone will be too distracted getting a New Year's Eve kiss to notice a little electrical fire, yeah?"

I snort. "No, see, it'll be too hot in here already from that, we don't need any more heat adding to it!"

We laugh, and my mind wanders to Ivan. I haven't heard from him all day. He hasn't said anything about plans for tonight. Maybe he isn't much of a New Year's kind of guy?

That's going to make tonight hard to dance around, I realize, as Natalie peers down at me mischievously.

"So, Katy, with business up again, are you gonna let yourself cut loose for a kiss? You'll have the lion's share of the men tonight, after all. They'll practically line up for you."

"Somehow, I don't think 'make out with a club owner' is on the top of many people's New Year's resolution lists, Nat." I narrow my eyes with a smile and divert the question, "What about you? 'Hot bartender with a hot ride' reads as pretty kissable to me."

"Pssh," Natalie dismisses, climbing down from the ladder and helping me fold it up. "I don't need to wait for a special occasion, I can get some action whenever I want."

Ashton snickers in the back while Charlie looks up with a grin. "Speak for yourself. Boss, I've been thinkin' about this idea I've got, 'kiss for a cover charge,' kind of like a happy hour. You think tonight I could..."

"Alright," I raise my voice, though I'm unable to hold back a smirk, "don't forget we're going to be WORKING tonight, everyone. Be ready to take numbers and get lucky AFTER we're rolling in the New Year's Eve income."

The crew mumbles a vague assent, and the decorations proceed through the morning.

But every few minutes, I can't help but check my phone. There's a lot at stake tonight, both for the club and for me.

* * *

TECHNICALLY, the club has a maximum capacity. Tonight, I'm pretending like it's at least double what it is every other day of the year. I'm the boss, I can do that.

The Amber Room is so packed I can hardly see over the crowds of people from the elevated stage on the north side of the club.

I'm in a short red dress for the evening instead of the usual black. It isn't that different of a cut, but even while I'm staying professional, I want to start the New Year with something a little, well, fresh. My shoes are jet-black and my lipstick matches the dress, so between my heels and the platform, I feel like a queen surveying my dominion as I lean on the leather couch, having just greeted a couple of VIPs who are enjoying the stage. The VIP lounge was already booked up long before tonight.

I can almost feel the floor shaking under the rhythm of the dancers jumping to the DJ, who happened to be one of Brooklyn's up and comers, if Natalie's word was good. And it usually is.

That isn't the only thing drawing the crowds, though. Some of that extra cash went to advertising, and I made sure not to hold back for tonight. This may as well have been a grand re-opening.

The bar is barely visible over the sea of people, now well into their drinks, but I can make out the top of Natalie's head as she, and her new hires we were able to afford, frantically move around the bar. Under her watch, I know I don't have anything to worry about on that end.

I feel a genuine smile break past my natural anxiety over the busy evening. I never realized how much that money would help, but it's been more refreshing than I ever could have hoped. Even if its source does make me a little nervous when I remember it.

Midnight is approaching, and I'm admittedly a little excited to see how the partiers enjoy the light show. I had to go home to get ready for my appearance tonight, but Natalie stayed behind to rig a few surprises that even I haven't seen yet.

Just as I'm thinking about trying to wade across

the crowd to get to a drink, Ashton bustles up the stage, delivering a few martinis to the VIPs and winking at me.

"So, you pick out your New Year's special for tonight yet?"

I give her a chiding smile. "Oh, I'm sure something will come along, just stay focused on raking in the tips for now."

"Laaaame," she says, scooting closer to me and leaning in so she doesn't have to shout the conversation. "You know, there's a truckload of models here tonight, and I just know a few of them are looking your way. Do you even know how gorgeous you look? You KNOW dozens of guys out there want to be the power couple with you tonight."

She grins and I roll my eyes, but as I open my mouth to reply, I notice my cell phone light up in my purse, and I pull it out.

It's a text from Ivan.

"VIP lounge."

I look at the message for a few moments blankly before it clicks, and my eyebrows go up.

"Whassit say?" Ashton chirps as she sticks her head over my shoulder curiously, and I hide the cell phone against my chest.

"None of your business, that's what!" I tease. She makes a pouty face that I imitate, and she cracks up before waving a hand.

"Alright, alright, just don't let business be the first

thing on your mind when midnight rolls around!" She disappears into the crowd, and I breathe a sigh of relief and look at the text again.

Casting a glance around at the crowd one last time, I discretely make my way to the VIP lounge.

My heels click through the illuminated hallway as I make my way to the lounge. It's not as grandiose as the main floor is, but it's a comfortable, reserved atmosphere. I'd assumed a private party had rented out the place in advance, so the lights were kept dim enough for an easy, familiar atmosphere.

Suddenly, I start to worry. What if Ivan had wanted the VIP room to himself? What if he's in there right now, arguing with the patrons that already paid for it? My footsteps quicken as I round the corner, by now expecting to see a full-blown fight happening at the end of the hall...

...but as softened music from the DJ played through the speakers reaches my ears, I see only Ivan sitting in the lounge facing the hallway, setting up a couple of fluted glasses next to a champagne bottle and setting them on the floor beside the couch.

He looks up as his ears pick up my footsteps, and that easy smile crosses his face again.

"You're quicker than I expected," he remarks, standing to his feet.

"I..."

I have no idea how he slipped past me without my noticing. He's wearing a slim-cut suit as deep and stormy blue as his eyes, with a tie as black as the ceiling in the lounge. He strikes a starkly contrasting image to the orange room, yet he complements it like the centerpiece of the whole place.

"Ivan, I had no idea you were—"

He puts a finger to his lips, stepping forward slowly as his eyes take me in. I obey, letting my purse slip into a chair as he comes close to me with hungry eyes.

"You're more beautiful than the day I first laid eyes on you," he says, putting his hand on my arm and letting it run down its length. He takes my hand and gives a slight nod to the couch, leading me there with a gentle tug

"This is a new outfit," he points out.

"I've had a little extra spending money," I say back with a shy smile, and he guides me to sit down on the couch across from him. "I didn't know if I'd hear from you today, but—"

I'm quieted as he lifts my bare leg into his lap, running a warm hand up my thigh while his other hand unfastens the clasp of my shoe, letting it clatter to the ground.

"Did you think I'd let you say goodbye to this cold year alone?" he says in a low tone as he does the same to my other foot.

"Whatever you please," I say, my voice steady but my heart pounding.

Ivan tilts his head to the side. "You're uneasy, I can tell."

"Not because of you," I'm quick to backpedal, "these past couple months have been...absolutely unheard-of for business, I had no idea this place had so much potential to—"

"Katy," he hushes me with his voice, powerful hands massaging my tense calves, "Katy, listen to yourself. I don't have to touch you to know you're wound-up."

I lower my eyes bashfully, but he leans across the couch, turning my chin back up to meet his gaze, to which I obey.

"I want to make this evening something special. Soon, it will be a new year. I will see to it that you'll want to remember this one more than the last," he says, reaching a hand into his coat.

He withdraws a black silk blindfold.

My heart flutters, and I realize I'm instinctively biting my lip.

"I think this might help block out some of the distracting annoyances, no?" He stands up, leaving me draped over the couch, eyes even on him as he moves behind me and lowers the blindfold.

"All you need to do is take it off, if you wish, or tell me to do so. I won't refuse you." A smile spreads across his face again. "It would be no loss for me to see those beautiful doe eyes again."

That smile is the last thing I see before the cloth darkens my world.

My hands grip the edges of the couch in anticipation as I hear the sounds of his clothes coming off. I have no idea what he has in mind, and with my eyes shrouded in cloth, I'm entirely subject to his direction.

Strong hands feel up my sides and at his guidance, I wiggle out of my dress as he slips it off my shoulders, leaving me exposed on the couch before him. I can feel a flush in my face, and I bite my lip. I've never brought this kind of action to work. Ever.

Hell, I've never even changed clothes at the bar, and now I'm lying on a couch in nothing but the lacy underwear I put on this morning. I'm totally exposed, and my heart flutters at the thought that anyone could walk into the private lounge and see us like this — I didn't lock the door behind me, I was in such a rush to get to Ivan.

"You're still nervous," I hear Ivan's voice say as he guides my hands to rest up above my head, his other hand slipping around the back of my neck. My mouth parts, but I suddenly realize my body is too excited to compose a response.

"Let me help you relax," his rumbling voice orders, and I feel his mouth at my neck. I try to recoil from the feeling, but I feel his grip on my wrists tighten, holding me in his power with a single hand while the one on my neck teases me to expose more, let more of myself open before him as he sucks at the sensitive skin.

Then his hand slips down my neck and to my back, where I feel my bra being unhooked. Ivan tosses the fabric aside, then slips my panties off me with the same dexterity.

He backs off a moment, but I can feel his gaze bearing down on me. I'm strewn out over the couch, now totally naked save for the black cloth over my head, and I realize my heart is pounding its way out of my chest.

"What are you going to do to me?" I breathe.

"Making you mine," comes the response from the figure looming over me.

He rips my thighs apart forcefully, holding them up and opening my cunt before him like prey. I expect the feeling of his cock ramming into me, but I let out a yelp as the feeling of a tongue stroking my lips sends electricity through my body.

I can hear his moaning from below as he tastes me, the powerful muscle stroking my labia and making its way towards what it really desires, what it's searching for as though it was trained to seek it out.

The strokes of his tongue make me want to recoil at first, to hide from such sensations that I haven't felt in so long, but the more I wriggle, the stronger I realize his grip is on me. He can do whatever he wants with me.

I let out a sharp, short cry when the tongue brushes my clit.

Like a hunter, he dives in and attacks relentlessly, tormenting my sensitive nub with short, powerful lashes that send warmth through my body.

It isn't a sensation I could get by masturbating, I realize. He's so irreverent of the restraints I put on myself, as though he knows just the right motions to send me spiraling toward orgasm when I'm ready to push myself over that crest, but he has none of the hesitation that forces me to draw it out longer.

It isn't long before I feel myself getting wet by my own accord, and my breathing gives away how close I am to coming. This is all happening so fast, and in such an exposed place, that my body utterly surrenders itself to Ivan's whims. I can't help but be obedient to him.

"Just a little more, just like that," I beg him, and as soon as I do, I feel my thighs drop and his tongue retreat. My heart skips a beat, thinking I've done something wrong, and I almost want to lift the blindfold, but Ivan's fingers are already gripping my chin. His hot breath washes over my face as he speaks in a low, growling tone.

"You will come when I allow it, *moya zvezda.*"

His lips press against mine, his tongue invading my mouth and making me taste my own honey. I press my body up into him, my hands starting to wrap around his sides and feel his bare skin, but he presses me back down and begins to suck on my exposed nipples, pinning my arms up against the arm of the couch as he does.

Every part of me is electrified with sensation, and my body is dizzy with the stimulation.

He wants that.

"Please," I beg him, "please, Ivan, I want you to fill me so badly, I'll do anything."

"Yes, you will," he states, and before I can react, he's gripping me by the hips and hoisting me up. The next moment, my hands and knees are being pressed upon on the surface of the coffee table in the middle of the room.

I know what's about to happen, and as I brace myself on the hard surface, it dawns on me that he didn't set the drinks on the table when I walked in. He planned on this, on using me. I hear the tearing of a condom wrapper from behind me.

A cry escapes my lips as his hard, condom-covered cock slides into me from behind, and almost instantaneously I want to collapse on the table, barely able to hold myself up with my hands.

He starts to pull me further onto him, rocking back and forth until my pussy envelops his cock entirely, tight and absolutely wet.

My knees are already starting to hurt as he begins to pound into me mercilessly. I feel some-thing on my hair, and my head is tugged back as he grips it like a leash.

He's blocked out my vision, put me on a hard surface, and now he's holding onto my hair, putting me all the more under his power, but God, the way his cock is hitting the inside of my needy cunt makes me want to open myself all the more to him, to arch my back and shove myself onto him more.

"God, oh God," I gasp as the bulging crown within rams the inner walls of my womanhood, "Ivan, please...!" I can't even articulate my plea, but there's no denial in my voice: I want what he's giving me. I need it.

Ivan is silent, bucking harder and faster into me. I can hear some kind of commotion loud enough to penetrate into the VIP lounge, and suddenly my heart turns over. Is someone coming in? Now, of all times? *No!*

"Is — ah! Is someone coming?!" I hiss, but Ivan tightens his grip on my hair by way of silencing me.

"Come," he commands simply through his fast-paced bucking and grunts, and warmth fills my body as the excitement starts to become too much to bear. The feeling of restraint, the thought of random passers-by barging in, my needy cunt being denied what I so badly desire, I can't bear it any longer as the noise from the crowd outside becomes louder and louder.

A harsh groan bursts from Ivan as he comes, filling up the condom inside of me with hard pulses, and his wild thrusts send me toppling over my own orgasm, my arms buckling and letting my face press against the hard wood surface, mouth gaping and eyes clenching beneath the cloth as my whole body shakes.

Ivan is still hard and merciless. Even as jets of his seed fill up the rubber inside me, he torments my wildly ecstatic body, disorienting me with the sensation as I melt into a shaking pile of pleasure on the table, my knees slumping to the side as he withdraws his cock at last.

Finally, I'm able to make out the sounds from outside.

"HAPPY NEW YEAR!"

Ivan had made us come into the New Year.

As the cheering and music outside resumes, I hear Ivan's footsteps moving around the room, and I nearly have a heart attack when a loud POP makes me withdraw my limbs again, even as my fluids mar my table. I feel a hand taking off the blindfold and turn my helpless body over on the table.

My eyes adjust to see Ivan, smiling and shirtless, looking down at me affectionately with a bottle of champagne in one hand and two crystal glasses in the other.

He sets the glasses down and pours the liquid, then pulls the couch up closer to the table where I'm sprawled. Still regaining my senses, I feel his strong arms lift me up as though I were made of paper, carrying me over to the couch as he sits down with me in his lap.

I blink blearily, a smile crossing my face as I wrap my arms around his neck and let myself hang there, utterly fucked silly. His warm arms are wrapped around me, comforting my naked body as it tries to come down from the high of the orgasm.

I smell champagne as he brings a glass close to me, stroking my back with the other, and his mouth comes close to my ear.

"Happy New Year, Katy."

KATY

*I*t's surprisingly chilly when I wake up on Valentine's Day. There's frost on the windows lining the wall of my apartment, and my toes are almost numb. Shivering, I draw up my legs and slide out of bed, finding a pair of slippers and a fuzzy robe to wrap myself in. I look at the clock to see that it's just after ten o'clock in the morning. I'll have to start getting ready for work soon.

But first, I need my coffee.

I shuffle into the kitchen, yawning as I start the coffee maker and slump back against the counter. I squint across the room out the window and stare long enough to notice tiny, delicate snowflakes drifting downward. It's been unseasonably warm and rainy this winter until now. I ponder what the snowy weather will do for my business. It could keep everyone bundled up inside. Or they might possibly head out to the clubs and bars in droves, looking to warm up with a drink and a hot stranger. I hope it's the latter — business has been pretty good, but I'm not out of the woods yet. There are still debts my father left me, even if the protection fee from the mafia isn't an issue anymore.

Right on cue, my phone lights up with a text. "Natalie, that better not be you calling out of work to take some starry-eyed girl on a Valentine's date," I mumble to myself. Blinking in the low light, I read the name on the screen. It's Ivan.

As always, at any sight or mention of him, my heart skips a beat. I don't know what it is, whether it's nerves or fear or excitement... or something else.

I slide my phone open to read the text.

"Good morning. You're taking the day off."

I furrow my brows in confusion. Taking the day off of what? Work? Being a sex slave?

After a moment of thought, I reply with just a simple question mark. Almost instantly I get a response from him, and I can't help but crack a smile.

"It's Valentine's Day."

Who would have expected that a gun-toting, heavily-muscled mafia hit man was a sucker for made-up romantic holidays? Stranger things have happened, I remind myself. And besides, he has been surprisingly tender and sweet to me these past few months. The sex is often hard and fast and rough —

not that I'm complaining in the least — but in our regular interactions, Ivan is a lot gentler and more sensitive than any guy I dated in the past.

Not that I'm sure you can call what Ivan and I do *dating*.

Just at that moment, my phone goes off again with another text from Ivan, who has written, "You have a date."

"Do I?" is my coquettish response. I can't help but bite my lip and grin down at my phone like an infatuated teenage girl. This is ridiculous.

"Da, printsessa. I will pick you up at noon."

I don't know Russian, but I'm fairly certain Ivan has just called me *princess*. Part of me wants to be indignant, tell him off and inform him that I'm nobody's little princess. But the bigger, more dominant part of me is just flattered. After another minute of staring at my phone with my thumb hovering over the keyboard, I finally sigh and set the phone down on the counter.

After all, I have a hot date to prepare for.

Totally neglecting my freshly-made coffee, I all but skip to my bathroom to take a shower. As I shampoo my hair, I imagine the inevitable conversation I will have to have with Natalie and the crew about why I'm not at work today. I can already tell she's going to give me hell for it. And I can't really blame her. I was all prepared to bite her head off if she dared ask me for the day off! But, I reason with myself, if she really is dating Ashton, then at least being at work will also allow her to hang out with her girlfriend.

So, really, I have nothing to feel bad about!

I blow-dry and curl my hair to create subtle waves, and then I stand looking at my naked body in the mirror, the fog slowly clearing away from the mirror's surface. I turn and look at myself from every angle, wondering what exactly Ivan sees in me. Sure, I'm decent-looking enough, I suppose. But I'm boring. Or, at least I must be in comparison to the kind of lifestyle Ivan leads. With his sharp good looks, money, and dangerous charm, I'm sure he can get any woman he wants.

Why me?

I put on some soft pink lipstick and smoky eye makeup before standing in front of my closet staring pensively at the clothes hanging there. I'm realizing that I have no clue what kind of date Ivan is taking me on.

"What the hell should I wear?" I wonder aloud. Finally, I decide on a knee-length, flouncy lavender dress, thick leggings, a khaki pea coat, and a purple woolen scarf. I check the time and realize it's now almost noon! So I tug on a pair of brown boots, grab my purse, and head downstairs to the lobby to wait for my rugged, Russian mobster date.

I stand near the entrance, looking out the window at the snowy scene outside. There isn't a whole lot of snow on the ground yet, but the people walking by are bundled up in light sweaters and scarves. I can see puffs of air when they breathe. Finally, a chilly New York winter day, after months of dreary rain! My phone vibrates in my hand and I look down at the text.

"Come outside."

I walk through the doors to stand on the sidewalk looking around for Ivan.

My phone buzzes again. "Look left."

I glance to my left to see a big white taxi cab pulling up to the pavement. I start walking over to it when the back passenger door opens and Ivan steps out, dressed the most casually I've ever seen him. He's wearing dark, neatly-pressed jeans, a grey sweater, a perfectly-tailored black jacket, a steel-blue scarf, and black oxfords. He looks absolutely delicious. Ivan reaches out a hand to me and I take it, meeting his dark-blue gaze a little nervously.

"You look radiant," he says, his voice deep and gravelly. I give him a smile.

"Thank you."

Something from my childhood, my mother warning me not to get into strange cars with bad boys, flutters in the back of my mind. I brush it aside and let Ivan help me into the taxi. I've already done a thousand things my parents told me not to do — might as well add another one.

"So, where are we going?" I ask brightly.

Ivan reaches over and places a hand on my thigh. "A beautiful place."

"That's not very helpful," I reply teasingly.

"Just wait and see."

We ride along for about an hour, and I'm wondering how expensive this taxi ride is going to end up. With my financial struggles, I try to avoid cabs unless absolutely necessary, resigning myself to the buses and subways. But glancing at the fancy clothes Ivan is wearing, I am reminded that he can absolutely afford it.

We drive up through Brooklyn and Manhattan, occasionally getting stuck in traffic for a few minutes here and there. It's a mostly silent drive, except for the small talk Ivan makes with me, asking about the club, about the burgeoning romance between Ashton and Natalie.

"I love that you've noticed that, too," I laugh.

"It's incredibly obvious. They aren't exactly trying to hide it, are they? If so, they aren't doing a very good job of it," Ivan replies, a smile warming his face. It's remarkable how drastically a simple smile can change his countenance. When his lips are in that hard, resolved line, he certainly looks the part of a hit man. But as soon as he smiles, he looks like Prince Charming. It's a bizarre and intoxicating dichotomy, and I can't help but want more.

"I hope they aren't mad at me for not coming in today," I admit, the guilt weighing on me. After all, I am the owner. If I can't show up to work, how can I expect anyone else to?

"I spoke to Natalie about it last week," Ivan says breezily.

"You what?" I retort. Ivan gives me a raised eyebrow.

"I knew it would burden you, but you need this day off. So I told Natalie you would be out today. She took it very well. In fact, I think she enjoys getting to be the boss when you're not around. Might want to watch out for that one," he jokes with a wink.

I sit stewing for a couple moments. I'm pretty independent and private, and the last thing I need is some guy to swoop in and make my decisions for me. I like my freedom. And like he said, I *am* the boss. I shouldn't need a man to come in and talk to my employees for me!

Still, I can't pretend it isn't kind of nice that I don't have to worry about it. I do so much, and I am in control of so many things. Sometimes it really does feel good to have someone else take the reins…

"You're angry," Ivan remarks astutely.

"Not angry, exactly."

"Offended?" he pushes. I wish he would just drop it.

"It's just that I like being in control," I admit quietly. Ivan squeezes my thigh.

"And I certainly do not want to take that control

from you against your will, Katy," he explains in an undertone. "But I think you like it more than you say."

Again, there's that mingled sensation of irritation and arousal. What does it say about me, a strong woman with a hold of her own destiny, that I enjoy being bossed around and dominated by a bigger, stronger man?

"You may be right," I reply softly. The car finally slows as the driver parallel parks on the street. I look out the window to see that we are at the American Museum of Natural History.

"Well, here is our destination," Ivan says, smiling again as he pays the driver and takes my hand to assist me out of the cab. "We're going to see the butterflies."

All my previous annoyance dissipates instantly. I can't help but laugh out loud. This has got to be a joke — going to the Butterfly Conservatory with my Russian mafia hit man master.

"Don't you like it?" Ivan asks, and the twinge of slight insecurity in his tone almost makes me melt right there on the icy sidewalk. He actually cares if I like his date idea or not.

"I love it," I reply genuinely.

We spend the next hour or so wandering through the bright flowers and butterflies, shedding our cold weather layers in the near-80 degree temperature of the conservatory. It feels like a tropical paradise, a slice of warm, colorful heaven smack dab in the middle of snowy New York City. I feel like an ethereal being, floating around surrounded by such beauty. It's truly a magical place, and I find myself feeling a little dreamy as Ivan guides me by the hand, excitedly pointing out different moths and butterflies.

But my stomach is rumbling by now, and Ivan suggests that we go to a sweet little café down the street for lunch. It feels exhilarating to walk down the street hand-in-hand with such a powerful man. Despite the precarious, transactional nature of our relationship, and despite knowing exactly what Ivan has done with these hands, I still feel safer than I've ever felt.

And yet that underlying current of danger remains, and I like that, too.

When we get to the restaurant, he firmly informs the hostess that we want to sit in the front corner. She takes one look at him and immediately acquiesces. It doesn't take much for Ivan to get whatever he wants. All he has to do is fix you with that cold, forceful gaze.

He orders a sandwich and a vodka tonic, while I eat a bowl of pasta and sip my peach martini. I keep wondering when the cutesy-date portion of our day will end and my Prince Charming transforms back into my domineering sex master.

As lovely as the past few hours have been, I have

to admit that I am starting to really anticipate the inevitable second part. He's staring out the window wistfully at the snow, looking as though his mind is a thousand miles away. I wonder if it really is.

"You like the snow?" I ask conversationally. There's a moment's delay before he replies.

"*Da*. It reminds me of home."

I feel a little blindsided by this sudden glimpse of Ivan's inner thoughts. He's usually so closed-off and cold, it's hard to imagine what goes on inside his head. I wonder if he will mind if I push him for more information...

"Russia?"

He nods. "Balakovo."

"I imagine it's a lot colder there, though," I add.

"Yes. Much colder. And quieter. Much smaller than New York. It is where I grew up, and sometimes I still miss it."

"How did you end up here in the Big Apple?" I prod. Ivan stops and looks at me sideways, causing me to freeze up instinctively. I hope I haven't asked too much.

"It is a very long story, and not a happy one. I am sure you don't want to hear it."

I nod, looking at him expectantly. I am sure that he is about to tell me no, that it's time to leave. But instead, after a few moments he waves over the waitress and orders another martini for me and a vodka on the rocks for himself. Once the new drinks appear, he takes a long sip and then leans in closer.

"I was just a small boy when my mother and my older sister Anya were killed," he begins, swirling the vodka gently in its glass. I prop my chin on my hand to show that I'm listening.

"I don't remember it at all because I was only three, but the witnesses say that four men on motorbikes forced my mother's van off the road and into a ditch. My mama, she was killed instantly, and poor Anya bled out before the policemen and the doctors came. She was eleven. We were driving to visit my father at work."

"I am so sorry," I murmur to him, a little breathless. His story sounds so similar to mine — the way that my mother and brother died. He continues.

"My father came to take me home from the scene. You see, he was a member of the *Spetznaz* — the special forces in Russia. He was a very tough man, a well-trained soldier who could kill a man as easily as look at him. But he was also fair and gentle, and he lived his whole life in the light. He was a good man, Katy, working within the law."

"Who were the motorcyclists? Did they do it on purpose?" I ask.

Ivan nods gravely, a dark look crossing his face. "They were very bad men. My mother and Anya did nothing to provoke them. Their deaths came as revenge for something my father did. He was part of a unit trying to take down the mafia."

The confusion must be obvious on my face, because he immediately adds, "Yes. My father opposed the mafia. He was instrumental in capturing and dismantling the mafia's hold on a small town on the Siberian border, for which they never forgave him. It was just a minor village, and my father was just doing his job, but they could not accept the loss."

"So then, what did your father do?"

"He did not retaliate. You see, he could not. He was now a single father with a very young son — if anything were to happen to him, I would have been an orphan. And Russian orphanages are not good places," Ivan explains. "But he did one thing that the mafia did not expect. He raised me to fight."

Ivan pauses to take another draught of his vodka. "My poor father, he realized that it was not enough for him to be a fighter. He had lived his whole life thinking he could protect his family, that he was enough to keep them safe. But the day of the accident, he learned otherwise. No matter how hard we try, evil can always strike behind a turned back. He learned that he would not always be around to shield me from harm, so he had to teach me to protect myself. And he did. Do not get me wrong, my father was always a kind man, but he was also very disciplined. He did not allow me to cry as a child. He taught me to hide my weaknesses and to grow my strengths. I could hold a gun and shoot a target from a distance by the age of seven. I could get my father in a headlock and bring him to the ground by my fourteenth birthday. My father was a good soldier, but he trained me to be even better."

I am utterly enthralled with Ivan's words, sitting rapt and quiet, as he sips his drink and shakes his head sadly. "I was going to join the *Spetznaz*, myself, when I came of age. But when I was sixteen, something terrible happened."

"What?" I prompt, on the edge of my seat.

"My father died."

"Was it the mafia?" I ask in a near-whisper.

He gives me a mournful look. "No, *moya zvezda*, it was a natural death. Old bones, long winters, and a broken heart are the cruelest killers."

"Is that when you decided to come to America?"

"Ah, the story is not that simple. You see, when my father died, I nearly lost my head. Finally, thirteen years of pent-up rage boiled over and now there was no one left to keep me in check. So, I prepared myself for a mission: to find the men who killed my mother and *sestra*. I did not sleep for many nights, spending every minute in pursuit of their names and addresses. Turns out they were all old men by then, but they kept themselves very well-guarded. One day, I tracked them all to a lounge in

Novosibirsk. I managed to subdue the guards and get inside.

"I told them who I was. I made them confess to their crimes. And then I executed them, one by one." Ivan takes another drink and sets down the empty glass. "But I was still a lawful man, Katy. In the middle of that bloody scene, I started to call the police to turn myself in. I knew I was guilty, and I had no reason to hide anymore."

"What happened?"

"Before I could dial the number, I heard the sounds of guns clicking from every direction. I looked up to find myself surrounded by members of the mafia. They'd responded quickly to the threat and now they had an ultimatum for me."

"What was it?" I ask, my eyes wide.

"They gave me two options: to die, or to join them. Automatically I chose the first option, but then they mocked me, telling me how despicable it was for me to allow myself to die, throwing away everything my father had worked for. They called me a coward."

"Wouldn't it have been easier for them to let you turn yourself in?"

Ivan shakes his head. "They did not want the police involved any more than necessary. So, finally, I gave in. I joined the mafia. They were so impressed with my skill that they trained me as an *ubiytsa* — a hit man. They wanted me as far away from the

Special Forces as possible, making me cut all ties with Russia, so they shipped me off to Brighton Beach. I have been here ever since."

I finish my martini with one big gulp, completely at a loss for words.

Ivan fixes me with a serious, almost regretful expression. He is so handsome.

"I understand if this changes the way you see me, Katy."

KATY

I reach across the table, place my hand on Ivan's wrist earnestly, and he locks my eyes in the deepest, most entrancing gaze. He slowly, delicately lifts my hand to his lips and presses a gentle kiss to my knuckles. I feel my heart tripping over itself with excitement. Ivan does not take his eyes off of me, does not lower my hand, but raises his other hand to snap his fingers, getting the waitress's attention. She hurries over, and I can all but feel her tension as she witnesses the smoldering heat between us at the table. *Poor girl*, I think. *You're standing too close to the flame.*

"Ready for the tab?" the waitress asks meekly after a moment.

Ivan nods, then finally breaks away for just a second to reply, "Yes. We are."

"I'll get that right now, then, sir." She rushes

away, undoubtedly blushing. I, however, feel surprisingly cool. Something has shifted between Ivan and I over the course of our time at this table. I know him better now, better than perhaps anyone else. I don't imagine that Ivan is the sort of man to share just that sort of personal detail with just anyone. I have gotten the impression that he lives a solitary kind of existence — without friends to confide in, without family to remember him as he used to be so long ago.

He has shown me his own heart, even just for a short moment.

And now I want — no, *need* — him to show me another side of him, a different part.

He pays the bill, leaving an overly-generous tip, and leads me out the door by the hand. We step out into a sudden swirl of snowflakes, the air so cold it momentarily takes my breath away. Just as I gasp at the temperature, Ivan pulls me close and seizes my mouth in an engulfing kiss, his hand clawing at my hair, trailing down to clutch my ass. With my lungs tightening in my chest, I feel an inexplicable euphoria. He pulls back to stare hungrily into my face.

My throat opens and immediately I inhale sharply. Ivan raises an eyebrow and cracks a slow, somewhat diabolical grin. He's no sadist, I know, but he seems to be taking a unique pleasure in depriving me briefly of air. And I have to admit that I kind of like it, too.

"What do you say we get somewhere warm and lose these clothes?" Ivan growls huskily, moving close to breathe the words into my ear, sending a shiver down my neck.

"We've got a long drive back," I reply, unable to repress the slight pout in my voice.

Ivan kisses me again, harder this time. "I have a place much closer."

He snakes an arm around my waist and tugs me down the street to hail a cab. Even in the heavy snow, it only takes about ten seconds for a driver to take notice and pull over for him. I wonder what it must be like, being so riveting and powerful a figure as Ivan. The world seems to fall hushed in awe at the sight of his stature, the sound of his voice. Being at his side, I feel as though I'm in the presence of a power I have never touched before. And if I just stay with him, I get to share in the glory of it. Like I'm made bigger, stronger, almost invincible beside him.

We climb into the cab and Ivan gives the driver some quick instructions, and then we're off, winding quickly through traffic, peeling off down side-streets. I halfway wonder if Ivan slipped him something, we're going so fast. But I can't worry. I physically can't bring myself to give a damn about anything but the desire rising in me, the need to be impossibly close to the impressive man seated beside me. Luckily, he seems to feel the same way.

Ivan turns to me and entangles both hands in my

hair, pulling me to him in a kiss. Before I can stop myself or think better of it, I clamber over to straddle him in the back seat of the taxi cab, never breaking our kiss. Ivan slides his hands down my back and down over the slope of my ass, giving it a quick smack. I moan into his mouth and move closer, my crotch coming full-flush against his. I can feel myself getting aroused, even through the layers of clothing separating our bodies.

"Soon, *solnishka* — my sunshine," Ivan whispers to me, smoothing my hair back from my face with a delicate tenderness. "My place is nearby."

Just a minute later, the driver announces, "Stop's up here on the right, sir."

"Fantastic. Pull to the curb, will you?" Ivan says.

The driver obliges and stops the car alongside the pavement in front of a swanky-looking gray marble building I don't recognize. I've lived in this city nearly my whole life but this is an unfamiliar area for me. This ridiculous city never ceases to amaze me, and neither does Ivan.

Once again, Ivan pays with an over-the-top gratuity to the driver, and helps me gingerly out of the cab, taking care not to let me step in a slushy snow-covered puddle on the way out. He all but lifts me over it up onto the curb. I smile into his face, which is ruddy-cheeked with the cold and decorated with fragile, tiny snowflakes. I cannot help but kiss him right there and then on the sidewalk, despite the cold, despite the passersby strolling past. I can't care less about the looks we get from anyone. All that matters is the warm, handsome body in front of me, and the way he makes me feel.

He hypnotizes me with that steely gaze again, holding me entranced in his arms as he sweeps me out of the snow and through the sparkling revolving doors of the building. Standing in a massive, immaculate lobby illuminated by a row of three glittering chandeliers, I can't help but spin around like a character in a romantic comedy on her first awe-stricken trip to the city. But I've never been anywhere this nice before, and the awe is genuine.

"This way," Ivan says, and he pulls me toward the elevator, past the front desk of smiling, beautiful women in form-fitting white receptionist uniforms. We ride the elevator up to the very top floor and step directly into a penthouse with wall-to-wall, floor-to-ceiling glossy windows. The furniture is smooth, shiny leather and the carpet is so plush that I feel my feet sink at least a centimeter as soon as I step onto it.

"It's… breathtaking," I murmur, my breath literally quite taken away.

"Take off your clothes," Ivan orders in a low growl.

Immediately, I strip out of my layers to stand in my lacy panties and bra. It's unceremonious and desperate, and I can feel goosebumps of excitement raising up on my skin. Ivan drops his jacket to the floor and rubs his hands together, staring at me with ravenous desire.

"This apartment is nice. But this," he says, gesturing with a flourish toward my almost-naked body, "*this* is breathtaking."

He rushes to me and lifts me up in his arms with such effortless ease, kissing me hard, his tongue pressing into my mouth. I wrap my arms around his waist and he pushes me up against the wall, pinning me there. I make a move to try and run my hands through his hair but he stops me, deftly pinning my arms above my head with one hand while his other arm holds me up. I am utterly amazed at his strength — I mean, I knew he was strong, but this is remarkable. I feel his chest muscles rippling against me and the place between my thighs responds with its own need.

Ivan leans in and nudges my head to the side to get at the soft, ticklish flesh of my neck, kissing his way down from my jaw to my collarbone. His full, luscious lips suck tantalizing love-bruises into my skin, marking me as his own, for all to see. The sensation makes me shiver and moan with pleasure. I need him more than ever, but he is taking his sweet time.

"Oh God, Ivan," I whimper breathlessly, "I need you."

"Not yet," he groans, tightening his grip on my

wrists above my head. It hurts just a little bit, but it only seems to add to the bliss of the moment, pain mingling with the delicious pressure of his lips on my bare skin. And he knows it.

"You like it rough, don't you, *mishka?*" Ivan whispers gruffly. He grazes my exposed collarbone with his teeth, eliciting a rattling moan from my lips. "Answer me."

"Y-yes. Oh yes, I do!" I sputter, my cunt growing slicker by the second. Something about his captivatingly authoritative tone, his unrelenting strength, the knowledge that he could crush me in an instant — it was totally intoxicating.

"You want me deep inside you?"

I nod and choke out, "Yes."

"Yes, *sir*," he corrects me.

"Sir," I add. He kisses me full on the lips and then lets go of my arms so that they fall at my sides. Then he kneels down slightly and hoists me up higher, without so much as a grimace, so that my legs come around his shoulders, his face level with my crotch. Moving back a little and leaning me back against the wall, he noses at my pussy through the silky fabric of my panties, and I cry out in surprise.

He glances up at me with a smirk, then tears the fabric aside with his teeth. He gently kisses my cunt, then begins dragging his warm tongue up and down, nibbling delicately at my clit, so that I buck slightly against his face. My hands clutch in vain at the smooth wall for something to grab hold of as he puts harder pressure on that little bundle of nerves. I roll my head back and shut my eyes, my breaths coming quick and short now.

I've never been so adeptly manhandled in my life, held against a wall with a tongue between my thighs. He's still completely clothed, and I'm so vulnerable and exposed, but that makes it even hotter. I reach down, blindly fumbling for Ivan's head, then finding it and gently, subtly pushing him into my cunt. He groans in what appears to be a "back-off" warning, and I immediately let go. He is in control. He's always in control.

To punish me for my transgression, he sucks at my clit, hard. The shockwave of pleasure tinged ever so minutely with tantalizing pain shoots upward through my body and I yelp his name, my heart hammering in my ribcage.

Ivan takes this as a sign of encouragement and doesn't back down, instead lapping harder and faster at the tingling folds of my pussy, swirling his tongue around my clit relentlessly. The feeling is so over-whelming that I almost want to shove him away and close my legs — but damn it, I can't. It is almost too much, but it still feels fucking amazing.

Besides, even if I wanted to, I doubt Ivan was ready to give it up.

The next moment, he pulls back for a breath, and looks up at me. "If you want me to stop, you can say so," he murmurs, his lips slick with my honey.

"Please don't," I reply quietly. He licks his lips and dives right back in, sucking my clit and rubbing it with the pointed tip of his tongue with vigor. The sudden reprisal of sensation electrifies my nerves and makes me moan, "Oh my God."

Ivan quickens the tempo, burying his face in my pussy until I feel my orgasm building rapidly, the pleasure ratcheting up and up until my whole body tenses — and then releases with a violent rush of bliss. Ivan becomes gentler in his motions, but still hungrily lapping up my juices as I come down from climax with a few shuddering twinges.

Then, in one fluid movement, he takes me down from his shoulders and carries my limp, sated body like a ragdoll down the hallway to a bedroom. I'm still dazed when he sets me down on a massive king-sized bed and begins stripping out of his clothes, dropping them in an unceremonious pile on the floor. When he stands tall and naked, the late-afternoon sun soaking every inch of his glorious flesh, I can't help but stare in awe and desire.

Finally regaining some sense of self after my mind-shattering orgasm, I scoot back on the bed and spread my legs open, watching Ivan expectantly. I want to call him to me, beg him to fuck me, please and now. But he holds me under his spell, and I am quiet, waiting.

At long last, he walks over to the side of the bed and lies down beside me, his huge, glorious cock pressing against my thigh. I ache with the need to have him inside of me, pushing deep into my cunt, filling me up. I want to tell him so. But I resist — I know he will only fuck me when he's good and ready.

He pulls me close, turning me away and rubbing his cock against my ass. His thick, strong arm reaches over my side to massage my breast, taking the nipple between his thumb and forefinger and drawing light circles around it, causing it to stiffen. The sensation makes me breathe raggedly and thrust back against him, moving my ass up and down along his shaft.

Ivan groans, the low sound vibrating down the back of my neck. He pushes my hair out of the way and peppers my shoulders with gentle, teasing kisses.

"You want me," he mumbles imperatively.

"More than anything," I reply, my voice barely more than a whisper.

"Tell me." Ivan gets up and rolls me back onto my back, positioning himself between my legs. His cock brushes against my clit in the process, and I inhale sharply.

Looking up at him dazedly I reply, "I want you."

"Beg me for it," he orders.

"Please, sir. I want you inside of me now. I want

you so bad I can hardly stand it," I answer, with complete honesty. I don't even get a chance to be surprised at myself, because then Ivan is leaning over to kiss me. He sweetly caresses my cheek, his thumb swiping down the curve of my jaw.

"Good girl," he says, with true affection warming his voice. With one more kiss, he reaches for the nightstand and retrieves a condom, starting to unwrap it.

In another move totally out of character for me, I reach up and boldly stop him from opening it. I bite my lip and lift my hips to brush against the head of his cock.

"Please, I want to feel you inside me — *really* feel you."

Once the words are out of my mouth, Ivan instantly tosses the condom aside and wordlessly positions his shaft at the entrance of my cunt. I hold my breath.

And then he pushes inside of me and my mind goes temporarily blank.

The feeling is so entirely overwhelming, so incredibly good, I can feel tears prickling in my eyes. The look on his face tells me that he feels much the same way. Ivan pulls back and thrusts into me, filling me so wholly with his beautiful cock. The feeling of his hot, soft skin moving inside me is delicious, and I can feel my toes curling. I close my eyes and moan his name as he pushes faster and deeper.

He's reaching that secret spot, hitting it perfectly with every thrust, and I know I won't last very long. Ivan pulls my legs up over his shoulders, allowing his cock to push even further into my pussy. He's so fucking big it almost hurts, but it feels so good that I honestly don't even care if he splits me in two. I just want him to keep fucking me.

"You feel so good, *malishka*," Ivan groans, the pleasure apparent on his face nearly enough to send me over the edge. "You're so fucking good."

Suddenly my orgasm is coming, and I start breathing heavily, my hips moving in rhythm with his motions. He can sense my impending climax, and starts fucking me harder, each push deliberate and deep. Before long, I cry out in bliss, my pussy clenching with waves of pleasure around his thick cock.

And he isn't far behind.

"Oh fuck, Katy!" he bellows, and with one final thrust I can feel him pull out and spurt a hot, sweet stream of come across my thigh. I can't explain it, but some part of me wants to cling to every last drop. I want him to mark me and tell me I belong to him.

And I realize now: I do. I belong to him, utterly and completely. And not just in the transactional manner, but in heart and soul.

I am his, for as long as he wants me.

He leans down to kiss me long and sweet. He lies

down beside me and I turn to face him, feeling his seed slowly drip down my bare skin into the sheets. Ivan is gazing at me with the same dark blue eyes that have stricken fear and obedience into many a hard-hearted man — except now his eyes are soft, almost docile. There is a sweetness in his expression as he looks at me, and then a slow, beautiful smile lights up his features. I am breathless.

I run my hand across Ivan's chest as we lie together, relief washing away any of the real worlds worries once again. I close my eyes for a moment, letting myself revel in the feel of his muscular chest, then down to his impossibly hard abs.

There's a silence between us for a moment, but it feels peaceful, somehow. It's as if both of us know not to speak, just letting the moment hang in the air lazily between us.

But my eyes open, and my gaze falls on the tattoo on his chest. An eight-pointed star, marking him as one of the Russian mafia's men.

Just like that, the magic of the moment is dispelled, and I'm reminded of my debt. Of the fact that I belong to this man. Whatever glue is keeping us stuck together... it's impossible to separate from the transactional nature of our relationship. It's not an equal partnership. As much as I want to justify our dynamic by allowing myself to feel for him, to long for him, I can never fully erase the fact that we would not be together under normal circumstances.

He's a mobster, Katy. Don't lose yourself to this.

But then again, since when has any part of my life qualified as "normal?" And besides, it feels good, damn it! Not just the sex — though, oh God does *that* feel good — but just simply being with Ivan feels good. The majority of the time we're together, it doesn't even occur to me that we aren't just a regular couple, even with his tattoos, his accent, and the nagging voice in the back of my mind, a voice I'm sure probably belongs to my dad.

If I'm going to belong to a hit man for a year, then I am for damn sure going to make the most of it, in whatever way I can manage.

"What are you thinking about?" Ivan asks quietly, his deep voice reverberating in his chest. I can feel the guttural vibrations of his words with my fingertips, and it's nearly enough to make me want to fuck him again. Almost. But I am so comfortable here, like this. Just being.

"Your tattoos," I reply simply. He peers down at his own chest.

"Do they bother you?"

I'm taken a little aback by the question. Ivan is certainly not the kind of guy to ask insecure questions — and he generally doesn't need to ask me what I do and don't like, either. He just knows. I pause for a moment and he seems to tense up a little, waiting.

"No," I begin. Then, thinking better of it, I add, "maybe a little."

"I would not have thought you the prudish type, *mishka*," he says, bemused.

"Oh no, it's not the existence of tattoos that bothers me," I respond quickly. "Maybe just the, uh, significance of them."

"Ah," Ivan says.

"It's just that it's a little scary, for lack of a better word," I explain hastily, hoping he isn't offended. *Good move, Katy. Offend your gun-wielding, heavily-muscled, Mafioso pseudo-boyfriend while you're lying naked beside him. Fantastic.*

Ivan lets out a rare, low laugh. I instantly breathe an internal sigh of relief.

"Well, I suppose that is to be expected," he says breezily. "In fact, I would be concerned for your mental health if you were not at least a little bit afraid of my associates."

I can't help but laugh, too, partly in relief and partly just at the absurdity of it all.

Ivan continues, "But, my *solnishka*, please understand that you need not fear them as long as you are with me. I can protect you. I promise you that."

He turns to look at me, a soft smile on his full lips. I snuggle into his side, feeling very warm and safe. It's not so bad, this relationship. Besides, I am getting a lot more out of this form of mafia protection than I was as just a debtor months before!

Suddenly, I find myself itching to confide in him the way he confided in me. I want him to know me, really know me.

"My mom and brother died, too," I murmur, with no preamble. Probably not the most tactful start to this particular conversation, but here we are.

Ivan sits up a little bit, turning his full focus on me. He furrows his thick brows and cocks his head to the side slightly. "When?"

I sit up, too, and shift around to face him, sitting cross-legged on the bed and pulling a pillow into my lap for moral support. "Many years ago," I reply. "And it was very much like the way your mother and sister died."

"Car accident?" Ivan prompts, looking genuinely interested.

I nod, fiddling with the hem of the pillowcase nervously. "Yes."

"Foul play?" he asks, the hardness returning to his expression.

"No, no. It was really just an accident," I answer quickly. "Honestly, it was."

Ivan runs a large hand back over his head. "Well, either way, it is a horrible thing."

"Yeah, it is. I wasn't as young as you, and I wasn't in the car at the time. But I still think about them every day, you know."

"You never really heal from that kind of wound," Ivan agrees.

I'm quiet for a moment, biting my lip. Then, the words just fall from my lips: "But I can understand their deaths. Unlike my father's."

Ivan takes my hand in his, gently rubbing the back of my hand with his thumb supportively. This gives me the strength to continue. "He was murdered a couple months before you met me."

"Who killed him?" Ivan demands, his rage suddenly bubbling to the surface.

I shake my head sadly. "I still don't know. There was a quick but thorough investigation, but they never did find out. It drives me insane thinking that the murderer is still out there living his life while my dad is gone. It just isn't fair."

I'm surprised at myself for sharing this much. I've never found the words to tell anyone else, not like this. But something about Ivan does this to me, makes me act like someone else, someone more open, less afraid.

So I go on. "I was away at college when it happened. I grew up here, you know, and after my mom and Steven died, I never imagined I would leave my dad. I couldn't just abandon him to run the club alone. But he encouraged me to leave, to go off on my own and live my own life. So finally, I did. And I was having so much fun, Ivan, just being myself, being a college girl. And then somebody killed my dad while I was gone."

I stop to catch my breath and swallow back the

lump in my throat. Ivan gives my hand a quick squeeze of encouragement and I resume the story.

"So I came back and I've been trying to run the club alone ever since. I don't want to let my dad's dream die, even if he did. The Amber Room is really all I have left of him, and if I can keep his dream alive then it's almost like I can keep his memory alive, too. And I just keep thinking that if only I'd stayed home like a good daughter, he wouldn't have died. Maybe I could have done something to prevent it, to save him—"

Ivan puts a finger to my lips and shakes his head. "You were not your father's keeper, Katy. Remember that. Dark things happen when we are not looking, and you could not have stayed here forever just waiting for it. That is no life."

I hang my head and blink back the tears in my eyes. I have to stay strong. I'm tougher than this. *Get it together, Katy!*

"I only wish I had known you then," Ivan continues thoughtfully. "But I was not even in America at that time. I was in Russia."

I raise my eyebrows in surprise, and he adds, "I was in prison, specifically."

"Russian prison?" I ask, wiggling closer. "What for?"

"For nearly beating a man to death."

My mouth drops open. "N-nearly?" I manage to croak.

"Yes. I would have killed him if that had been the mission. But no, I wanted him to live, as an example to his peers of what can happen if a man fucks with a member of the mafia family. He was a very bad man, Katy."

"What did he do? Who is he?"

Ivan heaves a sigh. "Well, let me start from the beginning. I was here in Brighton Beach when my superior informed me of a mission back in the motherland. My boss's daughter, Yekaterina, he was worried for her safety. She had fallen out of contact with her father, and he wanted me to find her. So I returned to Russia for the first time since I was sixteen years old."

"And did you find her?" I ask.

He nods gravely. "Yes, *mishka*. It took me nearly a week, because she was in a hospital, under a false name — the Russian version of a Jane Doe. She was unconscious for the first few days after I found her, but I waited. I sat by her bedside for three long days until she finally woke up. I comforted her, told her I was sent by her father, who was very worried. She confessed to me that she had been working as a prostitute to make ends meet, and that her last customer had abused her greatly."

"Poor thing!" I gasp.

"Yes," Ivan agrees. "She was in very bad shape, *mishka*. The man really, ah, what is the phrase? He did quite a number on her."

"What did you do then?"

"Well, at first she did not want to tell me the man's name. She was very, very afraid, you see. And with good reason. He is an extremely powerful man in Russia, the owner of a large and influential company, and she knew it was dangerous to cross him. But after assuring her that I would keep her safe, she gave me his name. And I found him that very night, while she slept in her hospital bed. I found him, and I hurt him. For every blow he inflicted on Yekaterina, I inflicted ten upon him. I wanted him to suffer as she suffered — only worse. Even the lowest man knows that it is unforgivable to harm a woman or a child, and I had to teach him that lesson myself."

"How did you get caught?"

"I dared to let him live. I wanted him to walk down the streets covered in bruises and blood and have all of his wealthy, powerful neighbors know exactly what he was being punished for, so that anyone who saw him would also learn his lesson: that to lay a hurtful hand on a woman is the most evil act a man can commit," Ivan says firmly, determination glowing in his dark blue eyes.

I have never been so enamored of anyone as I am of him in this moment.

After a moment, he continues, "So like a coward, he turned me into the police. Because he has such power, the Russian government gave me a harsh sentence, and so I wasted a long time in prison."

"And then you came back here?" I ask.

"*Da*. My associates, they sent me back the very day I was released, angry that once again I had drawn police attention to their business. But upon my return, my boss was very pleased. He promoted me, gave me more freedom than ever before. I had truly proven myself a real asset to the mafia."

Ivan leans forward and presses a kiss to my lips. "So you see, as long as you are under my protection, no harm will come to you."

I give him a big smile and I can feel myself blushing despite myself. "Thank you. For everything."

"And I swear to you, Katy, I will find out who killed your father. I will find the murdering coward and make him pay with his life for what he has done."

It's a shocking and — in its own way — sweet proclamation. Still, I tell him softly, "If you find him, please don't kill him. I don't want an eye for an eye. Instead, I want him to be held accountable for his actions. I want the world to know what he has done to my family. And besides, I don't want you to risk your own life trying to do this for me. Promise me that you will simply turn him over to the police, if you find him?"

"*When* I find him," Ivan corrects. "And yes. If it is

what you desire, then I shall allow the vile slug to live."

"Thank you," I reply, and kiss his fingers delicately.

With that, we both rise and get dressed. Night has fallen by now, and it's time to go home. Ivan hails a car and we ride back to Brighton Beach in the dark, my eyes drooping with exhaustion. As we roll down the neon-lit streets and shadowy back streets of New York City, I feel Ivan reach over and take my hand. I slump against his broad shoulder and drift off to sleep.

When we arrive in front of my apartment building, Ivan tells the driver to wait for him, and he all but carries me upstairs to my home. He lays me in my bed, presses a gentle kiss to my forehead, and the last thing I can remember before I succumb to sleep is his whisper of "Happy Valentine's Day."

IVAN

J wish I could say there were two me's. One, the tender man, who looks out for his woman at all costs. Who loves with all his heart and gives with both hands open.

The other, a cold blooded killer.

But that would be a cop out. The kind of flowery garbage some soft-skinned shit behind a desk would say to excuse himself of all the wrong-doing he's caused. A way to fire thousands of workers just before Christmas, or order the deaths of innocents, then head on home with a clear conscience.

My conscience is never clean.

I'm not two men in one body, I'm just a man. And like the countless men before me who did awful things in the name of a cause, I'll live with that dirty conscience by pouring my heart into the bosom of some soft woman.

My heart, but not my confessions. She can never know what I've done. I couldn't bear to see the reflection of that monster in her eyes.

It's those kind of thoughts that risk becoming a liability at moments like these. I push them to the side. Not to let the other-me take over, as some might say, but to be the hard-edged blade the moment calls for.

More men need to die, and I'm the instrument to make it happen.

This time it's a messy operation. There is no time for slow calculation. No single man to take out that'll make the whole situation better. No. This time a whole slew of men have to die, and there is no time for precision.

The Irish gangs are mostly out of the picture, their time is past. But these young freaks are hoping to make a go of it again, driven only by a young man's ego, and a passion for mischief. These six punks have left a swath of chaos, killing some low level enforcers working for the bratva, but also any witnesses or poor young women who happened to be so unlucky as to cross their paths.

"This city'll be ours before long, lads!" says their round-eyed leader. Some twenty-something young creep, who might not have an ounce of Irish blood in him, but who got these boys to go along with his raping and pillaging, thinking themselves some barbarians of old.

They cheer and yell in their squalid lair, some dingy rat hole in a building that's all but abandoned. It lays on the edge of some old dockworks that are the victim of de-industrialization. The ideal spot for some young criminals.

The top floor is where they gather for their party, a bunch of dirty heroin and some scotch -- because they can't even manage to stay consistent on what they are about. I could've called this in to the police, let them wrangle these punks up. But they'd have blown it. They'd have dispersed and gone on to commit more violent acts.

It ends now.

Six men have to die now, I remind myself as I stand outside their door. My street clothes gone, instead it's dark brown turtleneck and pants, gloves and hat. This is gonna be a fight, and I don't use messy weapons like assault rifles. It's a pistol and my knife.

I count the moments, watching through some cracks in the wall as they shoot up. Let them get themselves messed up for me. It's a gambit, it'll make them sloppier, but it'll also make them more unpredictable. My bet is that they'd have been a messy gamble at the best of times, so might as well dull their reaction.

"I gotta take a piss," shouts one, and my time is here. The door opens.

Springing out of the dark, I grab the blocky kid

about the neck, dagger to his throat as I spin him around make him my shield.

"Shit!" one of them screams almost exactly in time with my gun. I was looking to take out the leader first, but instead I get one of his underlings. That head explodes into a mist of blood against the wall and he goes down.

That's four now, five counting the one in my arms.

"Throw down your weapons!" I shout, but I'm no cop and I pop another punk's head open, taking no time to watch the gore. There'll be no prisoners.

"Shit! He killed Jimmy!" cries one of the guys, and then I see him, the boss. That round-eyed lunatic looking wild with rage. I try to shoot him, but then the guy in my arms struggles and fouls up the shot.

They're starting to get their shit together and I slit the man's throat in my arm. He's a liability now, and the bloody, noisy death will hopefully distract them.

But it doesn't. These freaks have done far worse to many a poor young thing, they're immune to suffering. Only enraged because I've done in some of their backup.

Their leader pulls out a gun and fires, but I'm prepared. I was already ducking and retreating behind some ratty couch and the handgun blast goes wide. And though I want to take that shit-rat out, I have bigger concerns.

There's two other guys, and one is pulling out guns. He has a shotgun in hand and is pulling out another to toss to his friend.

Shotgun's are terrible. No dodging a shot from one of them at this range. So I put a bullet through the eye of the first guy, and now it's just me, the boss, and the 'lad' fumbling with a shotgun tossed to him.

"You'll pay for this you shit!" cries their leader, and he's pumping lead into the couch with no concern for how likely any of them are to hit me. None do, but it's a risk with each shot.

Sure, most of those potential hits would not kill me on their own. But even a grazing shot could make me flinch, and then the shotgun does me in.

I dive in close to Mr. Shotgun, jab my knife down into his shoe and he screams. The shotgun goes off.

But it's wild, thankfully. He wasn't aiming at anything, the squeeze of the trigger was probably the result of a spasm of pain from my knife slicing open his foot.

I roll and spring up behind the wounded man, but their boss is on point and fires. Luckily I've got about two hundred pounds of Irishman-wannabe between him and me, and I survive unscathed. The guy holding the shotgun though? Not so much.

It's one on one.

I fire a shot and for one of those rare moments I don't hit my target. Not directly.

I do, however, turn the right side of his neck into

a spray of blood that coats the west wall of the room in crimson. The 'boss' clutches his neck, big eyes now bug-eyes, as he watches me in horror, desperately trying to aim a shaky hand.

With a sidestep I avoid the shot, but it wasn't necessary, he wouldn't have hit me anyhow with that lousy aim. And I come in close, pushing that gun arm of his away from me.

"This is for that girl you did last Sunday, and all the rest before her," I say, and he watches in horror as I slowly sink my dagger up in beneath his jaw, through his mouth and into his skull.

It's better than he deserves. But life's not about what you deserve.

Otherwise Katy wouldn't be mine.

KATY

I wake up on a Wednesday morning to the shouts of people down along the streets. At first, in my barely-conscious haze, I feel panicked. I fall out of bed and rush to the window, afraid that perhaps a riot is taking place just outside my apartment building. But looking down, I see the throngs of people aren't angry — they're just a little drunk. Or a lot drunk, judging by the number of them holding huge pints of beer.

Of course. How could I forget? St. Patrick's Day is tomorrow.

Even here in Brighton Beach, with a great number of Russian people, St. Patrick's Day is a big deal, and people get really into it. In the years before my dad died, I may have taken advantage of the holiday for a little bar-hopping, myself. But nowadays it means one thing and one thing only: the Amber Room is gonna be *packed*.

And even though the holiday isn't technically until tomorrow, and despite the fact that upon looking at the clock I realize it's only 9 AM, all the local party crowds are already diving straight into the festivities. After all, there is a 24-hour liquor store down the street from my apartment complex. So naturally this early morning parade of drunkenness would occur practically right outside my window. Either way, I'm up now, so I might as well get dressed and prepare for the day.

In the past month, a lot of things have changed. For example, when I walk by my bed on the way to the bathroom, I run my fingertips along the firm, exposed backside of a Russian hit man. Ivan groans and turns over, rubbing his jaw with one strong hand.

"Good morning, sleepyhead," I say sweetly, bending down to kiss his forehead.

He smiles up at me, his blue eyes half-lidded with exhaustion. He has good reason to sleep so heavily — last night we must have fucked well into the early hours of the morning. My body is still sore from it, but I've never been happier. I'm moving into Ivan's place, and tonight is the last night I'll spend in my own apartment. In the meantime, we've been going back and forth between his place and mine, falling asleep beside each other every single night.

It's been absolute bliss.

"What the hell is going on out there?" Ivan asks, scowling toward the window.

"Tomorrow is St. Patrick's Day."

"Ah." He slowly gets to his feet and pulls me close to him to press a kiss to the top of my head, his hands rubbing their way down my back. I'm wearing a thin robe, and he is completely naked. I don't know if it's the chill in the March air, or morning wood, or what… but I can feel his massive cock hard as a metal rod against my thigh. I can't help but lean into him a little bit, nudging my leg against his shaft teasingly. I can feel little vibrations down my core when he chuckles, his chin still resting on top of my head.

"I hope you know what you're starting here," Ivan warns. I press harder into him, and he responds with a deep groan. "Damn, *mishka*, you didn't get enough last night?"

I shake my head and pull back to look at him. I know exactly what I want.

Luckily, Ivan always knows what I want, too.

He hoists me up and I wrap my legs around his waist, kissing him deeply as he carries me to the bathroom. Setting me down so that my toes curl on the freezing tile floor, he turns on the shower, then returns to me and slips the robe off my shoulders. Standing naked in the cold air, my nipples are stiff, goosebumps prickling on my flesh. But the shower quickly heats up and starts filling the little room with steam.

The two of us climb into the shower, standing under the hot stream of water, our bodies flush together. As the moisture slides down my skin, Ivan drags his hands down my back to squeeze my ass, pulling me closer so that his now-slick cock prods me in the thigh. Then he spins me around and tugs me into him, his shaft hard on my ass. Ivan reaches around with both hands to massage my breasts, toying with my nipples, sending little shivers of pleasure down my spine and to my pussy.

My shoulders instantly relax as I lean my head back, tilting to the side slightly so that he can kiss me, the hot water hitting our faces. I reach behind myself to take his shaft in my hand, firmly stroking him and running my thumb over the crown. I feel Ivan shudder with satisfaction at my touch and that alone makes me want him. Now.

I turn back around to face Ivan, and I stand on tiptoe to kiss him, his tongue pushing into my mouth, his hand coming around to tangle in my damp hair. Then I let him guide me down onto my knees. I kneel before him, almost as though in supplication

After admiring the beauty of his engorged cock for a moment, I lean in and pull the head into my mouth, flicking my tongue along the underside. I pump his cock with both hands at first, my lips and tongue worshiping the crown of his glorious shaft. Ivan is moaning my name, and it's the hottest thing I have ever heard in my life. His fingers are wrapped in my hair and I can feel him tugging at my head, trying to push me down on his cock. So I drop my hands and place them on my breasts, massaging my own nipples as I take as much of Ivan's shaft into my mouth as possible. He is so big it almost hurts, but I crave the sensation of his hard cock pressed against the insides of my cheeks. I bob back and forth on his shaft, my tongue dragging slick lines along the underside.

"Oh, fuck," Ivan grunts. "That's so fucking good, *kroshka*. Your hot, wet mouth…"

Encouraged by his words, I push myself further, taking him into my mouth until the tip of his cock brushes the back of my throat. I can't help but gag a little, and that only seems to stoke Ivan's desire, as he lets out a moan and tightens his grip on my hair. I pump up and down his shaft, sucking him hard. He's bucking his hips and murmuring my name and I know he must be close to coming.

Just then, he pushes me off and pulls me up to my feet again. Just as quickly, he spins me around and presses on my back to bend me over. Luckily, there is a lower railing for me to hold onto as he readies the tip of his cock at the entrance of my dripping cunt.

He rubs a teasing circle around my opening before growling, "Tell me you want it."

"Oh God, I want it so bad," I reply quickly, peering back at him over my shoulder and biting my lip. It's been long enough that I know what *he* wants, too. "Fuck me."

And then he shoves into me hard, my aching pussy enveloping his rigid, long spear. I cry out in pleasure as he grabs my hips and bounces me up and down against him, his shaft filling me up again and again. At this angle, bent over in the shower, he is able to perfectly hit that secret, sweet spot deep inside of me, and within a couple minutes I already feel my orgasm approaching.

"Oh God, Ivan, sir! Give it to me — oh God!" I wail, the delicious tension building rapidly.

"You dirty little slut," he murmurs between gritted teeth. His fingers dig into my hips and I find myself hoping they leave marks there. I love it when he fucks me rough like this. I love admiring my bruises and love bites later, being reminded of how good it felt to receive them. And just like that, I come with a little involuntary squeal, throwing my head back in delight.

"Good girl," Ivan croons, smacking my ass with a hard, wet slap. The stinging sensation only served to push me quickly into a second orgasm, which I released with another shriek.

My pussy gushes with honey and, still grasping

the railing with one hand, I reach down between my legs to massage my clit. "I want more, please!" I beg. "Don't stop!"

"What a hungry little cunt you have," Ivan groans, slamming harder into me with every thrust. He squeezes my ass and reaches to grab my hair, pulling it so that my head yanks back. His cock rams into my g-spot again and again while my own fingers rub my sopping-wet clit. "You want more? Ask and receive."

He picks up the pace, his cock spearing into me so quickly, so sharply, that I start to feel the good kind of hurt, and then I come for the third time. My pussy contracts around his cock and before long, Ivan's thrusts become frenzied and loses its rhythm.

"Fuck!" he roars as he rips his shaft out of me and spills a long stream of hot seed across my back. The act sends a rush of pleasure through me as it washes away with the hot water, and he massages his cock as he lets the rest of his seed pour out over my back. I'm in and out of a daze as I feel his hands, warm even through the hot water, massaging my sides gently as I push myself upright again and lean against the shower wall, breathing heavily along with him before he wraps me in his arms and we linger in the cascading water together.

* * *

I'M at the bar of the Amber Room with Natalie that afternoon, and she's pelting me with questions about what I'm suspecting is in store for me this weekend. It's still early, and there's hardly a soul to be seen out clubbing just yet, even if the St. Patrick's Day crowd is still gathering in the sports bars and restaurants already.

"Well," she rolls her hand in the air, asking for more. "What do you mean, 'dropping hints'? Are we talking Post-It notes on your lunchbox, or what?"

I roll my eyes. "They're *hints*, Nat, it isn't like he's spelling out what he wants to do for my birthday weekend." And it is indeed that time of the year again. The past few weeks had been peppered with, well, cute little dates. I didn't think this would be something I could expect from a criminal, but I have to admit, he's good at making me forget what he does.

"Well, it was the French restaurant one night," Natalie lists off, "and then he made you take that weekend off to go see some of the clubs uptown. So after all that, you think he's planning something special? What the hell does 'special' mean to him?"

"I don't know, but he seems to mention my birthday every now and then, so I can only guess he's got something in mind," I muse.

"Let's see," Natalie gets a playful look on her face, "are there any sports seasons happening? Maybe he'll take you to a game."

I wrinkle my nose, and Natalie laughs, obviously joking.

"Maybe out on a boat somewhere? Nice romantic tour over moonlit waters…!"

"Wish someone would take *me* out someplace nice like that," Ashton calls across the room as she passes by with a tray full of glassware to clean for the night.

"And what's your idea of a 'fancy' place, huh? You'd just want to go to Midtown as an excuse to go to the Olive Garden there," Natalie shoots back teasingly. Ashton scoffs and tosses her hair indignantly.

"Well they *do* have the best one."

After Ashton passes into the kitchen, Natalie rolls her eyes and lowers her voice to tell me, "I'm taking her to New Jersey next month."

I raise my eyebrows and tilt my head to the side, a grin spreading across my face. "Oooh, Atlantic City? *That's* romantic."

"No, asshole," she's quick to rebut, pawing at me in annoyance, but her face goes the slightest shade of red as she adds, "My family's down there, I want my parents to meet her."

I feel my face spreading into a wide grin, and Natalie suddenly becomes very interested in cleaning the bar and avoiding my gaze, even if there is a suppressed smile tugging at her face. There's a beat of silence before I break in.

"That's adorable, Nat."

"Shut up, boss."

As I open my mouth to antagonize my employee a little more, the doors open, and I see Ivan striding in with a smile on his face. The moment Natalie recognizes him, she smirks and ducks off to busy herself with something away from the two of us.

"Ivan," I start, stepping towards him with a smile, "you didn't mention you'd be dropping by today—"

I'm cut off as Ivan steps up to me silently, takes my hand in his, and slips a single rose into it, closing my grasp around it as he looks down at me with a gaze full of what I soon realize is quiet excitement.

He still looks stony, but there's a boyish energy under there I've come to recognize.

"Turn around," he says, and blinking, I obey.

"Ivan, is this part of some-"

"Shush, it's a surprise," he cuts me off, and the next thing I know, he's bringing the same strip of black blindfold from our New Year's night together up and over my eyes, blindfolding me right there in the club. It's not even my birthday yet!

KATY

$\mathcal{A}$ few minutes later, I'm sitting in the passenger's seat of Ivan's car and listening to the rumble of the engine as we go God-knows-where. Trying to lead me by the hand out of the club had worn out Ivan's patience pretty fast, so I'd ended up being carried out in his arms all the way to the car.

And he still won't tell me where we're going.

"Now, now, Katy," he chides after I ask him for what feels like the tenth time, "what good is the blindfold if you know?"

"Fine, fine," I pout, crossing my arms, "but seriously, Ivan, I'm not dressed for anywhere fancy, okay?" And I'm not exaggerating. I'm wearing tight-fitting jeans, a red spaghetti-strap top with black lace, and a black knitted cardigan since all I was expecting out of tonight was a routine evening at the club.

After what feels like an hour drive, we pull up someplace where the sounds of traffic tell me we're well into the city.

"Ivan," I start as he helps me out of the car before sweeping me off my feet again, "seriously, this is really sweet and romantic but—"

"But nothing."

He plucks the knot of the blindfold, letting it slide off easily and blinding me with the afternoon sunlight, but as my vision comes back to me and Ivan sets me back on my feet, I see what I've been led to.

We're in Central Park, and there's a horse and carriage standing expectantly in front of us. My jaw drops, more out of incredulity than anything else.

Oh. My. God. This has got to be the corniest thing in the entire world.

But despite myself, I'm covering a laughing smile with my hand as Ivan cocks his head at me, his heavy brow furrowing.

"You don't like it."

"No no, Ivan, I love it!" I laugh and wrap my arms around him, blushing half out of embarrassment and half out of how absurdly cute this otherwise terrifying man was trying to be. It was like he was studying romance movies just to figure out how to surprise me. Me! The girl that is technically his sex slave, but who he treats like a Goddess.

A few minutes later, the two of us are being wheeled around Central Park in the back of a carriage pulled like a couple of tourists fresh off the boat. Rather, Ivan is sitting in the carriage, and I'm squeezed into the space left over by his broad frame, despite his efforts to make room for me.

Sometime after I relinquish myself to being half-wrapped around his body in the seat to get comfortable, my hand is held in his. I look up at him with thoughtful eyes, and I see him looking out on the sights of the park with a genuine smile.

"So," I finally ask, "why the park, of all places? Doesn't seem like your usual style."

He thinks for a moment before responding, "In truth, I've never seen the place, for all the time I've spent around the city." He gives me a light squeeze and adds, "I wanted to share something new to me with you."

To natives, the park isn't much more than a place to be well clear of by sundown, but seeing someone genuinely taken with the place is kind of refreshing, in its own odd way. I look at him searchingly, like I'm trying to read into him as his dark blue eyes meet mine quizzically.

"Something on your mind?"

"It's just...I can't figure you out, Ivan," I almost

whisper, even as I hug his torso tight. "You do things like this for me that are so sweet I don't even know what to do, but then..." I twirl a lock of my hair around a finger, knowing I'm treading into dangerous territory. The stiff feeling of his arm around me tells me as much, but I press on, nonetheless. "Sometimes I think about what you do when you're away. Even when we're together sometimes, I notice when you leave the room to take some phone call, speaking in Russian. And those nights when you slip out of bed when you think I'm sleeping."

I'm looking up at him now, and his eyes are locked on mine with a warning gaze.

"Do not ask me about my work, Katy," he says evenly.

"I don't mean it like that," I breathe, putting a hand up to his face. He takes my wrist in his hand, and we're frozen there for a moment before I continue. "Where does this side of you come from, Ivan?" I finally let out.

Ivan's expression slowly begins to soften. A few months ago, this line of questioning would have earned me a sharp reprimand, but now, he lets go of my hand and lets it finish its course to his face, and I touch the hardened man's cheek as if it were a statue.

He closes his eyes a moment, then looks back out into the trees, where a few families are enjoying scattered picnics or walks in the fresh springtime air.

"Katy, I've always kept you well away from my... usual business."

He turns to look down at me. "I keep it that way because you bring something out in me that's different, Katy. I don't know quite how to say it, but I see things differently with you." He looks down at his hands for a moment, his brow furrowed as though he's struggling to find the words. "I do not regret the things these hands do. You know that. But when I'm with you," he looks back up to me, and I want to melt into his arms, "that feels so far away."

He suddenly straightens himself up a bit and rubs the back of his neck. "But I know this is only a transaction to you. To me — don't say anything," he cuts me off as my mouth opens to speak, "I don't blame you in the least. But even if this is temporary..."

He takes my hands in one of his before withdrawing a little gray box from his coat pocket. My eyes widen as he opens it, revealing a sapphire pendant hanging from a white gold chain. It's absolutely gorgeous.

"I just want to thank you for being my light, *solnishka*."

I gingerly take the pendant from him, holding it in my hands with awe and care, as though it's a newborn child or something. I've never touched something so beautiful, so valuable. The sapphire glitters in my palm and I stare at it open-mouthed, almost afraid to move.

Ivan chuckles, which breaks me out of my reverie. He takes the pendant from me and, holding it up expectantly, asks, "May I?"

After a moment of shocked hesitation, I nod vigorously and lift my hair off my neck so that he can reach around and fasten the necklace around my neck. I look down at the sparkling gem nested on my collarbone and have to stifle an embarrassed smile at how badly it clashes with my too-casual red tank top. It's sort of like putting a diamond tiara on a clump of dirt.

But when I glance up at Ivan, he's got this starry look in his eyes. Even though his mouth is still set in a hard line, the warmth in his shining eyes softens his whole expression. He might as well be beaming. "You are beautiful," he says.

I notice the carriage driver steal a look over his shoulder back at us, and he gives me a quick, unobtrusive wink before facing away again. Ivan kisses me slow and deep, his lips warm and expressive against my own. He cups my face gently with one large hand, and I can feel the callouses there from years of working, of fighting. Distantly, some part of me rails against the fact that these hands have been stained with so much blood, have wrung the life from many a body. But in this moment, in Central Park under the early evening glow, with the whole city in celebration… it's easier to ignore.

"Thank you," I murmur, my cheeks burning.

"Are you hungry?" he asks, eyebrows raised.

I nod and smile at him broadly. "Where are we going?"

Ivan puts a finger to my lips, reaches into his coat pocket, and pulls out the black blindfold again. I start to laugh and protest, but he shakes his head, a bemused look on his face.

"Another surprise?" I giggle.

"I am full of them," Ivan replies lightheartedly.

"That you are," I answer softly as he ties the blindfold around my eyes again. I feel him get up and move forward, and I can barely hear him giving some kind of command to the carriage driver, but I can't make out the words. The driver makes an affirmative grunt and the pace quickens. I can hear the horse chuffing and its hoof beats speeding up.

Several minutes later, the carriage pulls to a stop and Ivan gets up again to pay the driver. Then he takes me by both hands and guides me to my feet. I take a couple wobbly steps forward before Ivan scoops me up in his arms and lowers me out of the carriage with effortless grace.

He leads me for what feels like several blocks, and I just know people have got to be staring at us. A huge, hulking Russian guy leading a petite girl in a blindfold down the street has to be a bizarre sight to behold. But the embarrassment pales in comparison to my excitement. Honestly, I don't much care as to where we end up, as long as I'm with him.

A few minutes later, he murmurs into my ear, "Okay. We're here." He unties the blindfold and I stand blinking under the streetlamps, looking around in amazement and confusion. I know we're not far from Central Park, but beyond that I have no idea where we are. This isn't a part of town I can normally afford to visit.

"The bars and clubs will be full of St. Patrick's Day people tonight," Ivan explains, "but I doubt any of them will go here."

He leads me into an opulent restaurant, far too fancy for the way I'm dressed. The sapphire pendant is the only part of me acceptable in a place like this. I look around in stunned silence at the magnificent interior design, the high ceilings and low lighting. The burgundy and mahogany walls are lit by candles and intricate glass fixtures. There are motifs of bears and heavy industrial art decorating the place, and huge, multi-level chandeliers hanging from the arched ceilings. After a few minutes, I finally realize that this is a Russian restaurant, and I feel a rush of warmth toward Ivan. It makes me happy to know that he is so eager to share his identity, his heritage with me.

The maître d' does give me a look of slight disgust upon seeing my casual, low-quality clothes, but that disappears quickly after a withering glare from Ivan. After that, it's as though everyone in the restaurant catches on and realizes that if you mess with me, you've got to be prepared to tangle with Ivan, too. And nobody really wants to do that.

So they seat us at a corner table with a candle flickering in the middle of it. Ivan guides me through the menu, pointing out items that he used to eat as a young boy back in Russia. We both order vodka to start, and although I am normally not a fan of most liquor on its own, this is so high quality that even I love it. Mine is a vanilla vodka, and his is made with artesian water from Siberian springs. To be honest, I don't really know what any of that means, but Ivan appears to appreciate it, so I don't question it. He then orders us borscht, foie gras, braised duck, and several kinds of caviar I've never heard of before. I cannot even imagine how expensive this must be, but Ivan looks entirely at ease and I decide it's probably better not to ask.

Everything we eat is absolutely beautiful in its presentation and even more so in its flavor. I find myself utterly blown away by every bite I lift to my mouth, and warmed by Ivan's enthusiasm for it. Every different item that I try is met with an excited question from Ivan, wanting to know if I like it and what I think about it. And watching him eat is almost wonderful enough just on its own. I can tell that this food is more than just a meal to him — it's a taste of home, of a life he can never truly have again. He is transported back to his childhood for the duration of the meal, and it's a lovely thing to watch. I am seeing a different side of him, full of wonder and lightness. It's a sharp comparison to the usual cold, no-nonsense hit man the rest of the world sees in him.

I feel honored. It feels truly special to witness such a tender aspect of his character.

For dessert, Ivan tells the waiter to bring us cheese-and-berry blintzes, as well as a bottle of muscat wine from Napa Valley. By this point I am already so full that the idea of trying to ingest anything else is a little intimidating, but the pure joy with which Ivan greets the arrival of our blintzes renders me unable to say no.

"These were my favorite as a boy," Ivan says. "My father, he worked long hours, so when I was young he often had me stay with an old woman in our building. Her name was Galina, but I called her *babushka*. Grandmother."

"She was your babysitter?" I prod, hoping for more. It doesn't happen often, but I adore hearing stories from his past.

Ivan gives me a noncommittal head-shake. "More or less. But she was not paid by the hour like most nannies are here in America. Instead, my father paid her rent and many of her other expenses. She was, you see, closer to my father and I than a mere babysitter. She was the closest to a mother I can clearly recall. She was a very old woman, quiet and reclusive, and fragile. My father knew she was struggling to get by, and she had always been fond of me anyway, so it was an arrangement which benefited us all."

"That's so sweet."

Ivan smiles faintly. "I suppose so. And *babushka* made the best blintzes. I used to beg her for them. So when I made good marks in school, when I behaved myself, she rewarded me with them."

"What a good woman," I say. Ivan takes my hand and kisses it.

"One of the best I have ever known. She is the one who taught me to respect and protect women. You see, my father taught me to be a hard man, but Galina showed me how to be soft."

"Then I have a lot to thank her for," I reply. Ivan nods.

"She died when I was twelve. But she lived a very long, interesting life. She was ninety-one when she passed, you know," he adds proudly.

We spend the next hour or so talking and cuddling, slowly draining a bottle of wine between the two of us. By the time the bottle is empty, we are both heavy-eyed and happy. The sharp, intimidating hit man is still present in his rigid, upright posture, and in his occasional dodging glance. He is authoritative when he speaks to the restaurant staff, and his firm hand on my thigh under the table is a reminder of his strength and control over me.

But I see now, more than ever, the genuine human being beneath it all. And I adore it.

After Ivan pays the bill with a thick wad of cash that makes me a little dizzy to look at, he leads me out of the restaurant and down onto the street. He hails a cab and drives me home, stroking my hair and holding me close the whole way back to Brighton Beach. Somewhere along the way, I fall asleep, and when we arrive at my apartment building he lifts me out and brings me upstairs to bed. I try to wake myself up, certain that he will want to fuck me. After all, it's his prerogative to use my body however he wants.

But to my surprise, he merely kisses my forehead and tucks me into bed, leaving silently. For a few hours I sleep heavily and contentedly. Then there's a knock at my door around midnight, so I blearily drag my ass out of bed and trudge out to answer it.

When I open the door, I see a rough-looking guy holding out a single rose with a sheet of paper wrapped around it. In my sleepy mind I can't figure out why a flower delivery guy would be dressed like a homeless man, nor why he would make a delivery in the middle of the night. But nonetheless, I take his delivery and go back inside to examine my flower on my bed.

Sitting cross-legged in the blankets, I set the rose

on my pillow and unfurl the letter, a smile on my face. I'm certain it has to be from Ivan.

But as I begin to read the words on the page, I can feel the blood drain from my cheeks and the smile quickly turns to gape-mouthed horror. I throw down the letter and rush to my bathroom to vomit.

KATY

I am absolutely sick with disgust and despair.

My bathroom has been my bedroom all night, as I lay curled up in the fetal position on the cold tile floor. I stare up at the shower, thinking bitterly about our morning tryst under the hot water yesterday, thinking about how much things have changed over the past few hours, since midnight. Since I woke up to that knock on my door.

And that letter in my hand.

It's now crumpled across the floor, damp with my tears and balled up and unfurled multiple times in alternate fits of rage and denial. It can't be true. It just cannot be.

I've thrown up a few times tonight, this last night in my own apartment. I shudder as I realize that I'm supposed to move out today. I'm supposed to take all of my stuff and put it in a moving truck to drive it all over to Ivan's place. That big transition, that culmination of months of learning to trust him a little bit, of learning bit by bit the reality of his past... it's supposed to happen today. And this time yesterday I was over the moon about it.

Now, I just feel nauseous.

In fact, when my cell phone alarm goes off reminding me that the movers will be here in an hour or so, I am so overwhelmed that I get up and crawl back to the toilet to vomit again. I regret drinking so much wine and vodka with Ivan last night. But I know deep down it isn't the alcohol making me sick.

It's Ivan.

It's what he's done to me.

Standing up and flushing the toilet, I trudge to the sink to splash cold water on my face, hoping it will wake me up and give me some idea of what to do now. I gasp at the freezing water and dry my face on a decorative towel, glancing over at my hollow-looking face in the mirror. There are purplish half-moons under my eyes and my cheeks are still patchy and pink from the tears I've shed throughout the night. I can't seem to pull myself together.

But I've got to. The hours are winding down and I'm running out of time. Because I have a strong feeling that the movers won't be the only ones showing up at my house in a couple hours. Ivan will probably tag along to help load stuff into the trucks. To make sure I comply with the rest of his plan to control me and keep me close.

To keep me under his thumb and blissfully oblivious to the truth.

Anger boils up in my gut and I finally kick my ass into motion, tying my hair back in a no-nonsense knot on top of my head. I get dressed in jeans and a comfortable sweatshirt, throw a scarf around my neck, and fill a duffel bag with necessities. I slip on my sportiest sneakers, grab my cell phone, stuff the letter into my pocket, and prepare to head out.

But before I go, I pick up the single rose which accompanied the letter and toss it in the garbage. I take one last look around my apartment, then hoist my duffel bag over my shoulder and head down the hallway, locking the door behind me.

I know exactly where I'm going, and I don't think anyone will be able to find me there. Not until I want them to. I load up into my car and drive a couple hours outside of town, to a small, barely notable suburb. It's a quiet, peaceful area, far outside the 24-7 hubbub of New York City. It's where my father used to steal away when life got too intense. He was a very hard worker, but he still needed a place to clear his head. And even when things got rough financially, he never could let go of this place.

I finally pull up to a little cottage far back from

the road, following a long, curving dirt driveway to the front of the house. It's a very small, quaint structure with one bedroom and a little old fashioned bathroom, complete with an antique clawfoot tub and a standing mirror. This is where my father retreated anytime he needed to leave his life behind for a while. He quietly bought it soon after my mom and brother died, and nobody knew about it but him and me. Sometimes I went with him, and we would rent movies and talk about politics, history, and everything else.

It's a place that I strongly associate with both a crippling amount of loss, of stress, and of making peace with the horrors of the world. It's where I need to be right now.

I get out of the car and carry my stuff to the front door, fiddling in my purse for the key to open it. Then I fit it in the keyhole and the door creaks open with a low whine. It's freezing cold in here, after months of being sealed up without the heat on. My teeth chattering, I hurry to the little stove that heats the house and turn it on. Almost immediately the cottage begins to warm up and feel like home again. I roll up my sleeves and walk into the bedroom, left pretty much untouched since my father's death. Even when I did come here after he died, I made sure to sleep on the little pull-out futon instead of in this bedroom. It always felt too weird, too disrespectful to intrude upon my father's space, even if he wasn't around anymore. After all, this was always his hideaway — not mine.

Until now.

"Daddy, I'm sorry, but I really just need to lay down," I mumble aloud, as though he can answer me and give me permission. But there's no reply. And I just crumple onto the bed, peeling back the slightly-musty quilts and snuggling down into the pillows with my cell phone on the bed beside me. I reach under the sheets to pull the crumpled letter out of my pocket and look over it again, now that I'm in a safer place. It's quiet enough here that maybe I can gain a little perspective and figure out my next move.

It reads:

'Dear Katherine Foss,

I have information pertinent to your business. It has come to my attention that you are fraternizing with a very dangerous man. You know this. You may have even accepted the nature of his profession. You have learned to care for him, maybe even love him. But you have been deceived. You don't know what he has done. And if you have any respect for the man you once called father, then you will cease all contact with him immediately. Ivan Dragomirov is the man who killed him. He was not ordered to do so. It was not a sanctioned hit from the Bratva. Dragomirov killed your father for personal plea-

sure. If you want justice for your father's death, then you will turn his killer over to the NYPD. Consider this a warning from a friend. Act quickly, before he suspects something and kills you, too.'

I feel tears stinging in my eyes and I hastily wipe them away, once again crumpling up the letter and dropping it over the side of the bed. The letter isn't signed, so I have no idea who sent it to me. I assume it must be someone else from the mafia, since the writer seems to know a lot about the inner workings of it. Someone who knows Ivan and probably knew my father, too. Anyone who speaks of justice for my father must be an ally, I think.

Then again, Ivan himself swore to me to find my father's killer.

I sit up angrily in bed and cradle my face in my hands. To think that I allowed myself to believe him! To trust him! I let him lure me into a false sense of security, let him woo me!

And he really did woo me, I realize now. Despite everything I knew about his line of work, I truly cared for him. And where has it gotten me? All this time I have been sleeping with the killer of my father! I feel so dirty and disgusting. I have betrayed my own father for the sake of money and lust. How could I have been so foolish? All along I knew it had to be too good to be true, but I ignored my instincts. Well, now I am in a far worse position than I was before.

For who knows how long, I lay in the bed, my knees curled to my chest, alternating between bitter tears of heartbreak and anger so intense it makes me feel physically hot. I lay paralyzed with indecision, with fear, as it dawns on me that the warning in the anonymous letter might be true. If Ivan goes to my apartment to help with the movers and finds me missing, he'll immediately look for me elsewhere. He'll go to the Amber Room, I'm sure. He'll call Natalie, Ashton, Charles — anyone who might know my whereabouts.

With a cold, shaking hand I reach for my phone. He's going to call me soon, I'm sure.

And what will I do?

Before I can overthink it, I go ahead and shut off my phone. That way, he'll just get my voicemail over and over again, and there's no way he can track my phone while it's off. Of course, I have no way of knowing for certain that he would even attempt that, anyway. But at this point, I have to rethink everything I thought I knew about him. It shouldn't surprise me at all if he *has* been tracking my location using my cell phone signal. After all, he has always been able to find me easily, seeming to show up unannounced wherever I was. And I never really questioned it, as his presence was always welcome.

But I have to remember that now he is a hostile presence. And he has all the resources of the mafia to keep tabs on me and follow my every move. I take the battery out of my phone and throw it across the room. Now I'm starting to get a little paranoid.

What if he finds me here?

I mean, as far as I know he has no clue that this cottage even exists, much less where it's located and that it belongs to me. I have tried to keep it a secret from everyone — even Natalie. So even if he interrogates her... she won't be able to tell him where I am. *Oh God*. I hope he doesn't interrogate my friends.

The writer of the letter is right. Once I disappear from Ivan's sight he will start to suspect me. He will become angry. I've caught glimpses of that anger, and I absolutely do not want to be on the receiving end. I never thought I would be. He always reserved some modicum of generosity and tenderness for me. But only when I followed orders like a good girl.

And this... this was not something a good girl would do.

He's gonna be onto me as soon as he sees that I'm not at my apartment, and being on Ivan's bad side does not bode well for anyone. I know what he's capable of, and I know what he could do to me if he wanted to.

Especially knowing what he did to my own father.

Another shudder of nausea rips through my body as I remember every detail of my sex life with Ivan. The same hands that have cradled me, gripped me, stroked me to orgasm — are the hands which ended my father's life. I feel so betrayed, so angry, and so incredibly disgusted with myself. I should have known. Somehow, I should have caught on before now.

And he's coming for me, with his muscles and his guns and his pinpoint rage.

Suddenly, my paralysis breaks and I am filled with a buzzing energy as I throw back the bedsheets and rocket myself out of bed. I have to search the house for something to protect myself, some kind of weapon. I am trembling as I tear through the kitchen, digging through silverware drawers that haven't been opened in years, knife blocks with too-dull knives.

My heart is pounding in my chest. I can't find anything to save myself. I will be totally helpless when Ivan inevitably finds me. He's going to tear me from limb to limb. He's going to kill me like he killed my father — ruthless and cold.

There are tears in my eyes while I look desperately through my father's old things. Anything, even a wood hatchet or a fire poker, would be nice. But there's nothing. It's as though the house has been child-proofed or something.

"Come on, Dad," I mumble tearfully, "I know there's gotta be something."

In my frenzy, I accidentally drop a box packed

with old Polaroids and they scatter to the ground. I slump to the floor, sitting in the middle of a circle of memories. There are pictures of me as a toddler, my brother in his elementary school play, my mom baking cookies and poking her tongue out at the camera. My dad holding up a big fish with an even bigger grin on his face.

"I'm so sorry. I've let you down," I whimper, holding my face in my hands. Then, as though by magic, a lamp I clumsily moved to the edge of a coffee table during my search clatters to the ground across the room. I groan and walk over to it, careful not to touch any of the broken glass. The dusty floor-length tablecloth that's been covering the table is lopsided, and when I try to arrange it back into place, it just slips off the table entirely.

I gasp at what I see underneath the coffee table.

There's a gun.

At first my eyes refuse to believe what they're looking at. There's no way I just found a fucking gun just sitting underneath the coffee table I used to play card games on. I mean, I must have played a thousand games of UNO with my dad, sitting on the floor at this exact, innocuous-looking table. Carefully, slowly, as though in a trance, I reach my hand underneath the table to touch it.

The metal is ice-cold, and there's dust on the barrel, but it feels real. Too real. I've never handled a gun before in my life, and I'm not even sure I can figure out how it works. I'm half-expecting the thing to just explode at any moment like a bomb.

But then I realize that I have what I've been looking for, at least to some extent. This is certainly a weapon. Whether I can actually use it or not, it will definitely serve to make Ivan hesitate. All I have to do is pretend I know what I'm doing. That might just be enough to stall him while I call the cops or something. Maybe. I hope.

So I pick it up and examine it a little, my heart hammering wildly in my ribcage. This is the scariest thing I've ever done, and possibly the stupidest. But I'll be damned if I don't at least try to stand up for myself when Ivan comes to find me. I turn around and bend down to scoop up some of the Polaroids to take with me. If there's a chance I might die today, I want to revisit some sweeter memories before I go.

I move into the living area to watch the front door, sitting with the gun and a stack of photographs in my lap. I stare at the photos longingly, willing myself to somehow dive into the pictures and live in those worlds instead. I stay this way for what has to be several hours. There's no clock in the house (my dad always said that the cottage was his "escape from time"), and with my phone deactivated in the other room, I have no real way of knowing the time.

But the sun is low in the sky when there finally comes a knock on the door.

By this point, I am no longer shaking. I am calm and resolute as I stand up, letting the photos fall to the floor. I cross the room and unlock the door, then back away a few steps. The door pushes slowly open and Ivan is standing there in the doorway.

I lift the gun and aim it at his handsome face.

I don't say a word. Ivan raises his arms up over his head in surrender.

"Search me, if you please. I have no weapons on me. I would never hurt you, Katy," he tells me in a low, deliberate voice.

"Bullshit!" I burst, brandishing the gun. Ivan doesn't even blink.

"I'm telling the truth," he retorts. "Search me."

"Ohhh, no you don't," I reply, my voice shaking a little. "I'm not going anywhere near you, ever again. I know how strong you are. You're just itching to snap me in half, aren't you?"

"Katy, please. Let me explain."

"There's nothing to explain, Ivan!" I cry. "I know exactly what you are and what you've done, and there's not a damn thing you can say that will change it. You're here to kill me like you killed my father!"

Ivan shakes his head and holds up his palms in front of him. "You've got it all wrong, *mishka*, I swear to you." That affectionate term — I looked it up, it means a perfect woman — is like poison on his tongue.

He takes a step closer and I put both hands on the gun, holding it level.

"Don't go any farther or I swear I'll — I'll do it."

"You'll what? Shoot me?" Ivan says. "You're really going to shoot me in your father's cottage, Katy? How do you think he'd feel about that?"

Anger rises like hot steam in my chest. "Don't you dare mention my father. You have no right to say shit about him, you murdering piece of scum," I growl. "How do you think he felt about being killed in cold blood, huh?"

"You're right. I am a killer," Ivan admits. "Because it is my job, Katy. And I don't kill good men. I kill bad ones."

"Was my father a bad guy?" I demand.

"No, that's what I'm—"

"Exactly. And you killed him anyway. I know what happened. You didn't do it because you were ordered to. You did it because killing is nothing but a game to you. Taking a human life is nothing to someone like you! I bet you even enjoy it, don't you?"

At that, Ivan's jaw clenches and my own blood runs icy.

"There is no aspect of my job that I enjoy. I did not choose this life," he replies quietly.

"Oh, poor you. It must be so hard having all that money and power, being able to take out anyone who rubs you the wrong way. What did my father do to provoke you, Ivan?" I ask.

"Nothing. I never met him."

"There you go with the lies again!" I shout, my arms aching from having to hold the gun up for this long. "You were so careful to keep this hidden from me, you even made up that whole sob story about being stuck in Russian prison."

"That was the truth," Ivan protests, but I shake my head.

"You made me think you were some kind of fucking hero, Ivan! Going off to the motherland to save some poor beat-up girl from the big evil bad guy. I bet none of those people even exist, do they?" My rage is fueling me at this point, and even if I die tonight, I am determined to have the last word.

"Look them up. Research the case. It made head-lines in Moscow."

At this I can't help but laugh bitterly. "Oh, you're unbelievable. Or maybe just delusional. But I refuse to believe in those delusions anymore, Ivan, okay? You don't control me anymore and I know that just kills you."

"Put the gun down, Katy, before you hurt your-self," he pleads softly, genuine concern on his gorgeous features. There was a time when that look might have melted me, but not anymore.

"I mean, how sick can you be? You killed an innocent man and fucked his daughter! And what's even worse is that you fooled me into it. I never suspected a thing. I mean, sure, I have been afraid of you all along because of what you do for a living. But I never once thought, *oh hey, this guy I'm sleeping with might have murdered my father*. So, bravo. Congratulations. You really played me," I confess, and now the tears are rolling down my cheeks in hot streaks.

Ivan looks truly pained. The look in his beautiful dark blue eyes is filled with heartbreak. But it has to be an act. I know by now that he is a good hit man and a *very* good actor.

"And you know what, Ivan? You know what I don't get?" I start again, emotion making me voice sound all wobbly and weak. "You claim to only kill bad guys. But the world isn't that simple, is it? It's not black and white, like you said. Every 'bad guy' starts out somewhere. He probably has a family. Even if you don't like him, somewhere out there, there's gotta be someone who loves him. So when you kill a bad guy, do you think about that? Do you even stop to think about his family? What did they ever do to you?"

"It is not my place to decide right and wrong, Katy."

"But when you sentence them to death, aren't you playing judge, jury, and executioner?"

Ivan stares up at the ceiling. "No. I am *just* the executioner."

"Then how do you know if what you're doing is right?" I press him, my arms now tingling from the effort of keeping the gun held up.

"I don't!" Ivan explodes. "I follow orders, Katy! I do my job! But I try my best to seek out justice, not revenge. I want to balance the scales, *solnishka*, not tip them. But in the end I am just an employee."

"Then what is your excuse for killing my dad, huh?" I shoot back. "If you're just following orders then why did you go after him? I know for a fact that it wasn't an order. So, what, did you just decide to do a little freelancing on the side?"

"You are correct about that, Katy. The Bratva did not order your father's death," he agrees gravely.

"Then why?" I implore, my arms wide open. I don't even care about holding the gun anymore. I already know it's hopeless. I don't stand a chance against this man.

But Ivan doesn't lunge for me like I expect him to. Instead, he calmly explains, "The man who killed your father did not do it because he was instructed to do so. Your father was a good man, and he did nothing to deserve such a cruel end. His killer was not acting out justice. He was filled with misplaced rage and frustration, and he dealt with it the only way he knew how. I promise you, Katy, your father was a good man, and his killer knew that. Perhaps that is really why he wanted him dead. In this business, we are surrounded by darkness, by evil and danger. We do not trust anyone or anything but our own sense of right and wrong. And there are things we cannot have — peace, stability, love — it comes with the territory. We live between the black and white, Katy. We are the gray. It is our lot in life, and only as long as we can accept that can we survive. The man who did this... he looked at your father and saw all the things he could not have, and resented him for it. Envy is a monstrous thing, my love. It creates monsters out of mere men. This man did not take your father's life to balance the scales, to remove an evil from the world. He did it because he was jealous and angry and because killing is the only thing he knows how to do. Violence is his only outlet. And because he stepped outside the gray for a moment to stand in the light which does not belong to men like him — like me — your father died."

"Is that a confession?" I ask darkly.

"No," Ivan says firmly. His gaze is steely and true. "In fact, I can prove to you that I am innocent. After you told me of his death, I did some research of my own. Katy, I know who killed your father. And if you let me, I can show you the proof."

KATY

$\mathcal{I}$ can already feel tears in my eyes as the old VHS player starts to load the tape, like a sense of dread building up in the pit of my stomach. Everything in me wants to tear my eyes away from this, to just bolt out of the cottage and run away.

But I keep my eyes steadily forward, my knuckles white as I ball my hands into fists from the pent-up storm of emotion brewing inside me. I want to believe him. More than anything, I want to be wrong about Ivan.

The screen lights up as the tape begins to play.

I see Dad sitting in his office, now my office, shuffling through paperwork. I feel a tug at my heartstrings as I watch him, looking just like I remember him before leaving for college. This feels like watching a ghost. It feels wrong. At my side, I

211

can sense Ivan wanting to put a hand on my shoulder, but he restrains himself. Instead, he narrates through the silent footage.

"As you know, your father owed protection money every month," he starts. "Like you, he was always punctual. It was a close call, sometimes, but from what I've heard of him, he was as diligent a bookkeeper as he was a manager."

The next thing I see makes my heart plummet. The door of the office gets kicked open, and my dad nearly jumps out of his skin at who walks in.

Konrad. Oskar and Nic are close behind him, though they hang back as Konrad moves straight for Dad's desk.

"But sadly, he was assigned to collect from you," Ivan continues, "Konrad collected from your father. He used to be in charge of collections instead of Oskar, a fact he's still bitter about to this day. And just like with you, he got rough the one time your father was unable to make his monthly dues."

There's no sound on the video, but I can almost hear Konrad's horrid voice yelling at Dad.

"You went to college that year, and your father insisted on paying your tuition. That's what cut into his income just enough to bring him short of his dues. When your father couldn't make his payment, Konrad demanded a different form of compensation," Ivan says with disgust in his voice. "He demanded you, Katy."

My eyes widen, and I tear my eyes away to look up at Ivan incredulously. His stony gaze holds no deception.

"This was not the first time he'd made such an advance, the animal," Ivan says, looking back at the video ruefully. Konrad is still stomping around and shouting at Dad. "He has lusted for you for a long time. Your father hid it from you so well, but Konrad has been circling you like a vulture for years."

I want to vomit, and I put my hands to my mouth as I watch Konrad order Nic to turn the table over, sending papers flying everywhere as my dad stumbles backward away from them. Konrad takes him by the scruff of his collar and tosses him into the center of the room.

"Now, Konrad thought he had his chance at you. It would be you, or dire consequences."

A gasp escapes my lips as I see Konrad throw the first punch into my dad's stomach, and as he stumbles back, Nic catches him and holds his arms back while Konrad squares up for more pummeling. I want to turn away, but I owe it to my father to see the truth.

"Konrad demanded to know where you were. He was going to collect on you himself. Your father would not budge. They had already searched his house, but your father had been shrewd enough to hide which college you were away at. He endured terrible things, Katy."

Ivan's voice is a little thick as he watches my innocent father get tortured by the thugs that are now inflicting awful things on my dad. I can barely watch, cringing and feeling my gut wrench at every blow.

"Despite everything that happened, your father wouldn't speak. He was silent during the whole interrogation."

I bite my lip and feel tears welling up in my eyes as I see Konrad cross the room and take down a baseball bat Dad had mounted on the wall of his office. I finally have to turn my eyes away when I see him use it to pummel Dad's stomach.

"You don't have to watch this, Katy," I hear Ivan's thick whisper, but I foolishly keep my eyes locked on the screen.

Konrad's face is red, and he's clearly utterly lost his temper. His motions are wild and uncontrolled, and when he raises the baseball bat high and brings a fast, hard swing at the side of my dad's head, I reflexively shut my eyes and turn away, unable to hold back the sobs in my chest as I instinctively know what just happened.

I'm a trembling wreck when I feel Ivan's hand rest on my shoulder.

"What Konrad did was officially an accident, he reported to his superiors. He was never supposed to commit such an act. Covering Konrad's tracks before investigators arrived at the murder site cost them a lot of money. Paying off the investigators cost even more. It cost Konrad his position, which is why Oskar runs collections now."

Through teary eyes, I see Nic hoisting my father's body up while Oskar checks for a pulse, shouting something angrily at Konrad, and I can watch no more.

"Turn it off," I ask Ivan through a choked voice.

He obliges, and I hug myself, leaning over in my seat.

"How did you find all this out?" I finally manage after taking a few moments to muster the strength to speak in an even voice. "If all this is true, why did you imply you didn't know who killed my father when I told you about it?"

"There were only three men who handled your business before me," Ivan explains. "Oskar, Nic, and Konrad. A demotion like Konrad's is not a common thing, so I investigated." His serious face allows a small smile to form. "I wasn't joking when I said I know Konrad's dear old *matushka*. She was more helpful than anyone else."

"What do you mean?"

"The circumstances of this murder were incriminating enough for Konrad. He wanted this tape we're watching kept even more secret. If his superiors had watched this, his consequences would have been far more severe. So he kept it with him, lied to say that he and the boys had disabled the security cameras before beginning their interrogation. He kept it in a safe at his own mother's house, along with the murder weapon — your father's baseball bat."

I'm reining myself in better now, and my swollen eyes look up at him with determination, anger, and confusion. "So why is he coming after us now? Why me?!"

Ivan closes his eyes, his hand balling into a terrible fist. "The bastard knows we're together, Katy. It infuriated him from the moment I brought it up to our superiors, and the beating I gave them only soured him more. He's a petty, wretched man, and this was a feeble move to try to incriminate me. He thought you might go to the police with this letter and spark an investigation that would have me arrested."

I look up at him evenly for a few long moments, then I stand up, and his gaze down at me is open and sincere. All of this information has been overwhelming. I don't even know what exactly I want to do — punch him, kiss him, run away, or maybe all three.

Finally, I let out a long breath, glancing at the blank screen once more before speaking.

"I believe you, Ivan."

I can't keep myself from embracing him the next moment, and he receives me with his strong arms, warming me with a hug I so desperately need as he buries his face in my hair.

"I'm so sorry I doubted you," I say in half a sob.

"You had every right to, Katy," he whispers back, "you had every right to never speak to me again after being put through so much."

I pull back a touch and look up at him, my lip trembling before I feel a weight lift from my shoulders as I look at what I can now believe more than ever is an honest face.

"Let's go home, Ivan," I whisper.

ON THE WAY BACK, something feels different between us. There were always times when the silences between us held some kind of tension, like between the moments of fleeting bliss together, there was this reminder that I'm with him as part of a deal. A transaction.

But as we drive back to Brighton Beach in his car and I lean towards him from the passenger's seat, wanting nothing more than to embrace him, that tension seems just...gone. Like it was a spell that's been broken, and we can breathe freely together.

I look over at him, and despite looking to be deep in thought, I can see some kind of relief in his face as well.

He's a hit man. He kills people for a living. But...he loves me, doesn't he?

The realization hits me suddenly. He didn't have

to do all this. He could have left me to hide in my cottage forever, or until Konrad found me. But he came for me.

And I realize that I wanted him to, desperately.

I swallow the lump in my throat just as he looks over at me and speaks.

"There's something on your mind."

I nod quietly, then look forward at the road as we drive closer to the place that feels more like home than anywhere else in the world could.

"Konrad is still after you, Ivan. After us. What happens now?"

"You're right," he nods grimly, "he isn't going to stop." He then looks at me with a cool, steady gaze that at once thrills me and raises the hair on the back of my neck.

"That's why I took the liberty of showing this tape to my superiors. They agreed with me on what needs to be done."

My face blanches, and I feel my hands go cold at the implication. "You mean…?"

"Konrad needs to be dealt with," he says with finality before looking at me again, "and I'm going to need your help."

My mouth is dry, but something else in me is stirring. Determination. I look at Ivan, the cool confidence with which he's approaching this, and I want him so badly in this moment. I want him to pull over and fuck me in the back seat of his car, but

I know that will have to wait. I have a family to avenge.

"Well, hit man?" I say with a feeling that thrills my whole body, "What do you have in mind?"

"Konrad is passionate for you. Mad, really," he explains. "Such lust-ridden men act irrationally, viciously, and impulsively. The sooner we act the better."

I nod, suspecting where this is going. "So we're going to set a trap for him, and you want to use me as the bait."

He looks at me with a tenderness and concern I didn't think to expect, and he hesitates a moment. "Katy, I wouldn't ask this of you if I weren't going to be watching over you the whole time. But I understand if you—"

"No," I stop him, resolution in my face even as I wring my hands, "I want this." Every part of me is trying to resist, but there's a part of me in the back of my mind fighting its way to the front, thrilling my entire body. I *need* this.

Ivan looks long and hard at me as we stop at a red light, then nods.

"Then listen carefully."

KATY

"*H*ello? Who is this?"

"Konrad, thank God! I don't have much time, I-"

"Wait, *Katy*? How did you get this number?"

I'm pacing around the club floor of the Amber Room. It's well before opening time, and I texted the staff ahead of time that we're opening late today to keep them out for a good long while. The only people here are me and Ivan, and he's pacing around at arm's length from me, listening to the conversation with hawk-like attentiveness.

"I got your message, Konrad," I breathe, desperation in my voice. "Oh my God, I don't know how much time I have before Ivan finds out I know, I-"

"Calm down, Katy, calm down," his horrible voice tries to coo, trying to sound reassuring and seductive but coming off as nervous and sleazy. "It's going to be okay, I'm here." I try not to grimace. He's been waiting for this call for so long, I realize.

I make a show of trying to take slow, deep breaths. "I...I took your number from Ivan's phone when he was in the bathroom. I'm at the Amber Room now, he's away on some kind of business." Ivan had told me some of his associates would back this story up. "Oh my God, Konrad, I'm so scared!"

"I know, I know, *mishka*," he tries to assure me, and I feel my blood boil as he tries to use the same pet name Ivan uses for me. "I knew this would be a risk for you, but I couldn't hold this secret while he was abusing you so monstrously, I had to tell you."

I have the phone volume up loud enough that Ivan can hear, and I see his face going red at the bile coming from Konrad's mouth.

"It's okay, Konrad," I breathe, "I...I can't imagine how I might have felt if I'd learned even later. Oh God, I've been living with a monster!"

"Don't worry, Katy," he says, "don't you think I thought ahead for this?"

Oh, I bet you did, you rat.

"What do you mean?" I ask, trying to sound as clueless as I can, going so far as to twirl my finger around my hair innocently. Ivan would be cracking up with laughter if he weren't trying to contain his anger at Konrad's brazen acts.

"I've had a car ready," he explains, "and I've been skimming money from jobs for months, enough to have a nice little nest-egg stashed away. All cash. And I know a man who owes me a favor; he's ready to give us new names, IDs, everything — new lives, Katy. We can disappear together. Ivan is a clever bastard, but he can't catch someone who's gone off the map."

The cruel smile on Ivan's face tells me Konrad's scheme would have gone off about as well as my father's 'interrogation' did, even if it weren't a trap.

"A new life?" I gasp, not wanting to sound too pliable, "Konrad, that would mean leaving behind *everything*, everyone I've ever known, and-"

"Would you rather stay here and risk the mafia's wrath?" His voice is suddenly sharp. *Typical. He's a textbook abuser. Sweep in to save the day, isolate me from everyone but himself, and get angry if any part of that goes wrong.*

"No, no, you're right," I assure him, sounding as demure and defeated as I can. "My life is in your hands, Konrad, I...I think you know better than me in all of this." I know he'll like that.

"Oh darling," I hear him rasp, lust building in his voice sickeningly, "I've waited for you to realize this for so long. Stay put, I will come over immediately."

"Please, hurry! I'll be waiting in the VIP lounge, none of the staff is here. I...I just needed some time alone. But I need to see you, Konrad, please!" I make my voice sound as needy as I can, positively dripping with desire, then end the call. Immediately afterwards, I collapse into Ivan's arms, shuddering.

He rubs his hands up and down my back, burying his face in my hair. "You did so well, Katy," he reassures me, and his deep voice is so much more sincere, so much more authoritative in its tone than Konrad's slimy lies.

I turn my face up to look at him with wide eyes, my fingers curling around his jacket for security. "I just cried for help from my father's killer."

"I couldn't have put on a better act myself," he says with a smile, taking my chin in his thumb and forefinger.

I smile, despite my nervousness, because I know he's going to be here for every step of our plan.

To say I'm dressed scantily is putting it lightly. I'm wearing my lacy red top that leaves the whole of my back exposed, and my black miniskirt shows off my legs in their entirety, all the way down to my stiletto heels. I'm wearing makeup, but not enough to make him suspect I'm gussying up for him too much. I have to look distressed, after all. I am, but not for the reasons Konrad thinks.

I feel like I'm putting myself out as chum for a shark.

"It's okay to seem nervous," Ivan strokes my back as we make our way to the VIP lounge. "Looking too confident is a rookie mistake. He's expecting a damsel in distress, he might suspect something if you throw yourself on him without restraint."

I nod. "And you'll be waiting to move as soon as he's...as he's on me?"

Ivan stops me just as we've reached the door to the VIP lounge. "I won't let him do a thing to you that you don't want." His voice has a deadly seriousness to it, and I look down, swallowing hard.

"I don't know if I can do this, Ivan. To...to actually kill a man."

Ivan just looks at me evenly, no attempt to persuade me one way or another in his eyes. He's letting me make this decision, I know. At long last, I raise my eyes again and give a hair of a nod.

"But I need this. As long as he walks free, he could hurt more people."

Ivan smiles at me, and there's reassurance dancing in his eyes. "I know you can do what you know to be right, *mishka*."

Ivan leaves to hide in the storage room, and I take my place on the couch. My heart is pounding harder than ever before.

* * *

It feels like an eternity before I hear a distant door opening, and dread fills my body.

No. I can't do this. I can't do this. This can't be happening. He's going to kill us both.

But then I remember Ivan, my colossal protector, looming over me with that easy command written on his expression and in his every movement, like a guardian angel with a star emblazoned across his chest. A certain warmth fills my chest, and take a deep breath as I hear the VIP lounge door swinging open.

Then my heart stops again as I hear *two* sets of footsteps.

A moment later, Konrad appears in the hallway, concern and lust intermingled in his expression as he steps into the room with arms wide.

"Katy, Katy, my darling! You're safe!" My blood curdles as I see the massive form of Nic lumbering in behind him. We hadn't expected Konrad to come with backup.

"Thank God, you're here," I breathe.

Even as Konrad rushes forward to me, he puts a finger to his lips. "Quiet, Katy, we aren't alone. Ivan may be here."

My face goes white.

"Wh-what do you mean? He's away on business!" I stammer.

Konrad shakes his filthy head. "I got a tip from one of my associates that this was a ruse of some kind. I think he knows you reached out to me, my darling."

There's terror in my eyes and my heart is pounding, but as Konrad approaches me and gingerly takes my face in his hands and looks into my eyes, he seems to think the terror written on my expression is out of fear of Ivan.

Konrad turns his head to Nic, who's already searching the lounge for Ivan, and nods. "Go find him. Kill him. You'll get your payment."

Nic wordlessly nods and heads out the lounge door, leaving me alone with Konrad. Immediately, he brings his mouth to my neck, his hideous mouth relishing my sensitive flesh. "Oh darling, I've longed for you to come to your senses for so long," he rasps, and it puts goosebumps on my body. His hands explore my form, dancing down my back and sliding around my hips.

"I'm so scared, Konrad," I whisper into his ear, trying my hardest to keep it together. It's an honest confession, at least.

"I know, my dear, I know, but you have nothing to fear. You're mine now."

His hands are groping my ass now, pulling me closer into him and pressing me against the little bulge in his pants. Suddenly I feel him trying to push me onto the couch, and I feel a lump in my throat.

"I told Nic to give us some time after he does the deed," he hisses into my ear, "I can't resist you any longer, and I can see you were thinking the same," he adds as he fingers my spaghetti strap, sliding it off my shoulder before ripping off my top.

The lust in his eyes is wild as he pushes me onto

the couch, licking his lips and unzipping his pants. My heart is pounding its way out of its chest, terrified of what's about to happen.

Nic is looking for Ivan. He isn't supposed to be here. This isn't part of the plan. He's going to take Ivan unaware, oh my God, Ivan's going to die and I'm going to be left alone here at the mercy of this monster!

Konrad takes my quick, short breaths as excitement as he penetrates my mouth with his tongue, and I feel his bare cock on my leg. He's really going to do this!

IVAN

*C*alm. Cool. Collected.

Those are all the things a killer needs to be when doing a hit. But how am I supposed to be calm when my woman is in danger?

What the fuck was I even thinking using her as bait?

I was out of my mind to give in and settle on that plan. I'd rather have to fight a hundred Konrad's -- no, a thousand! -- than put Katy in the path of one. Yet it's too late now. If I burst out now it could be at the wrong moment, and that greasy weasel could have a knife at her throat before I could shoot him.

I hear the sound of someone approaching too late, the first cost I have to pay for losing my cool. This isn't a job, it's my life, my love. And that's fucking it all up.

When the door opens I realize it's not Konrad,

but Nic. That blockheaded brute. That's about as bad as I feared it could be. I've seen this guy take a two-by-four to the head and not be fazed.

And I don't have a go-ahead to kill him, so my knife and gun are off-limits.

Only Konrad dies today, I tell myself. And I try to force calm, because whoever dies, it mustn't be Katy.

Nic's prepared, and as I come for him out of the shadows he reacts first.

He raises his gun and I snap my hands to deflect it, but it's a rouse. We're close and that big meaty fist of his strikes me in the gut. A kidney shot. Damn blow hurts worse than a bullet I once took.

But I can't react. Pain is just part of the flow, I remind myself. It's to be embraced.

I headbutt Nic, bashing my forehead into his nose, blunting it with a crack. And the big brute barely reacts more than I did.

He's too tough. The kind of mark I'd be cautious with. But caution has no place when my woman is on the line.

I grab hold of Nic's trigger finger and twist it away, making him groan in pain, but he punches me again and I am only able to dull it a little with my free hand.

"Time to sleep, comrade," I growl at him, taking a gamble as he drops the gun with a clatter.

Twisting his finger got him to drop the handgun, but that didn't help me much, because now he has two free fists to batter me. And he goes to town trying to hammer me with those fists immediately.

It takes all I've got to deflect and block his blows as the blood runs down from Nic's nose and into his mouth. And I know I can beat him. But in a battle of strength and melee skill, it'll take a while to wear down this brute.

So I have to take a gamble. Offer Nic something to wrap his hands around.

My neck.

I grapple with him until he takes the offer, and I feel him choking off my breathing, strength enough to collapse my throat in mere moments. But it gives me my clear shot.

I nail him in the gut as he expects, but there's little to be done to that brick of muscle, it just gets him to lean forward more. To open up my real target.

I have no kill order, but Nic does. And his eyes are full of murder as my face flushes with blood and the lack of oxygen begins to weaken my muscles.

Just one more hit, I tell myself.

Just one more.

I uppercut him in the jaw, and I hear teeth shatter as his head rockets back from the strike. I gasp for air as he staggers back.

It's not done.

KATY

"I'm going to make you mine before we leave," Konrad croaks, grinding up against me and jerking a hand up under my skirt, trying to rip my panties off. I'm almost dizzy with fear, and I know I have to act, fast.

I bring my lips up to his ear, brushing against it ever so slightly. "Let me get you out of that jacket, I want to *really* see you," I breathe, and he's too lust-ridden to refuse me.

He turns around, and with one hand, I trail my hand up his chest and to his collar, unbuttoning the top buttons and sliding the jacket down just enough to leave his neck exposed.

With the other hand, I slip between the cushions of the couch, searching for what I left there the last time Ivan and I fucked on this very spot. Then my fingers find it.

The black strip of cloth he used as a blindfold.

With every bit of speed I can muster, I yank the black cloth out and take hold of both ends of it, jerking it around Konrad's greasy neck and pulling and twisting as hard as I can.

There's a sickening gagging sound as I pull back with all my weight, and his hands immediately go to the cloth, trying to pry himself free.

"I'll-" he chokes, "I'll kill you, b-backstabbing **bitch!**"

"If I'd stabbed you in the back, you'd be dead already!" I shout back into his ear, pulling the cloth as tight as I possibly can. His face is starting to purple. *Just a little longer...!*

My hand slips.

In an instant, I see my life flashing before my eyes as Konrad uses that half-second lapse in my grip to rip the blindfold from my hands, tossing it aside and spinning around.

It's the most terrifying face I've ever seen in my life.

The next thing I know, I'm being hoisted into the air and tossed like a ragdoll onto the carpeted ground, sprawling onto my back and looking up at the enraged Konrad in terror.

"Fine," he spits, "if that's how you want to play it, you treacherous cunt, I'll *take* what your father owed me!"

He puts a knee on one side of me, and I feel his

hands wrap around my throat as he descends on me with murderous rage in his eyes-

CRACK.

I see Konrad's face go placid for a moment, then his grip lessens, and he slumps off me, and I see Ivan standing over him, my father's bloody baseball bat in his hand, fury on his face, and a trickle of blood running from a cut in his forehead.

Konrad rolls over on his stomach, clearly dazed, and he mouths something before Ivan grabs him by the neck, picking him up like a piece of trash with one arm, hoisting him up in the air with one hand. His eyes are filled with fire, and I'm paralyzed on the floor before the scene.

"I'll bury you with the rats that birthed you, *sookin syn!*"

Ivan's arms move like a flash of lightning, bringing the baseball bat over his head and crashing down in half an instant, caving Konrad's hideous face in with a sickening crunch. I turn away, covering my mouth after catching a glimpse, and a moment later I hear a second crack, and I glance back to see that Ivan has broken the bat delivering a second blow to the side of the bloody stub that used to be Konrad's head.

There's a moment of silence, Ivan staring at Konrad's body, me staring up at Ivan, both of us breathing heavily and petrified.

Then the splintered bat falls from Ivan's grip

with a clatter, and he turns to scoop me up into his arms, embracing me tight as I descend into sobs.

"Shhh," he whispers into my ear, his whole body warm and comforting as I break down in them, hands shaking and tears pouring from my face. "It's over, Katy, it's all over. Are you okay? Did he harm you?"

"Ivan," I choke out, "Oh my God Ivan, I thought you were...I thought he was going to—"

"He isn't going to do anything anymore," that thick, commanding voice states, and he holds me tighter in his arms.

"I had no idea Nic would be here," I manage, and he starts stroking my hair.

"I thought Konrad might have a friend to tip him off," he replies, "but I was surprised he would take such a risk. He must have been truly desperate. Nic is unconscious and restrained."

My eyes flutter open and look up at him in shock. "What?"

Ivan looks down at me steadily, his eyes utterly at peace with his actions as always.

"One life was sanctioned to be taken this morning. Nic aided a traitor, but he was not my target tonight, so I had to restrain myself." He turns his eyes back towards the lounge doors. "But truthfully, it would be a mercy to slay him now. The mafia's punishment for this action will be unthinkable." His eyes look back to me, brow furrowed in concern.

"But not so unthinkable as what Konrad almost did to you."

I nod silently as tears roll down my cheeks. I feel a strong finger wipe them away as gently as though he were stroking my hair. "Thank you, Ivan," is all I can whisper out, exhausted and shaken beyond belief as I hang limply in his arms.

His lips press into my forehead. "I would go to the ends of the earth for you, *solnishka*. Come, let's leave this place. The cleaners will be here soon."

Without another word, my hitman protector carries me out of my club, leaving behind all the baggage of my past and into what my muddled, tired mind thinks just could be a better future at last.

KATY

*M*y heart is pounding so hard I'm afraid it might actually jump out of my chest. I can hear my own blood rushing in my ears and I am gripping the sides of the leather passenger seat so hard my knuckles are bony-white. Ivan is driving my car away from the scene of the crime because I am obviously in no place to get behind a steering wheel. It's around noon and we are headed into the city, retreating to Ivan's place. I feel like every nerve in my body is electrified; I am hyper-aware of every tree and car we pass. I'm staring out the window, deep inside my own mind, trying to remember to breathe like a normal person.

"Relax your jaw," Ivan says, and his voice makes me jump a little. He glances over and gives me a sympathetic look. "You're grinding your teeth. Going to give yourself a nasty headache doing that."

"S-sorry," I stammer, massaging my jaw self-consciously. I hadn't even noticed.

Ivan reaches across the console and places a warm, comforting hand on my thigh, giving it a squeeze. "Don't apologize. You're okay. Everything is fine."

"W-what's going to happen now?" I ask, turning to him and searching his face for answers. I stare at his rugged profile, that gently hooked nose and sensuous lips. A smile twitches at his mouth.

"Nothing you have to worry about."

"Are they — is the mafia going to take care of the, um, the…"

"The body?"

"Yeah," I choke out. Ivan pats my leg and takes both my hands in his.

"Yes, *mishka*. They will take care of everything. The worst is behind us. The Bratva are very efficient at what they do. I swear to you, the place will be even cleaner than it was yesterday by the time they're done with it."

"And Natalie?"

"She will never have any idea that anything happened there at all. I strongly advise you not to tell anyone about what you saw today," he adds. "It is safer that way."

I nod quickly. I have absolutely no intentions of sharing this experience with anyone else for the rest of my life. I am taking the events of today to my grave.

"I could never tell anyone without incriminating myself. I mean, I was there. I had a hand in it. I am guilty," I say slowly, as though trying to convince myself of the reality. It's strange, I don't feel like I expected to. I had anticipated overwhelming guilt, hysterics, maybe denial. But instead I feel strangely relieved. My father's killer is dead.

"No, Katy," Ivan replies solemnly, looking over at me with a very emphatic gaze. "You are guilty of nothing. As far as the mafia is concerned, you weren't even there. And we will defend that statement with our lives. Even if we were to be discovered somehow — which will not happen — you will never be mentioned. You are entirely innocent of this, *moy sladkiy*."

"But I was there. I helped you… kill a man." I breathe the words softly. There is an audible sense of wonder in my voice. Part of me wants to address this now, go ahead and scream my feelings out, go ahead and enroll myself in the many years of therapy I should probably get. But an even bigger part of my consciousness is just glad it's over. I feel like a massive burden has been lifted from my shoulders, like I've finally completed a task I've been putting off for far too long.

"You did well."

"You think the mafia will hire me, too?" I joke weakly.

Ivan chuckles. "No, *mishka*. I don't think you're quite cut out for a life in the shadows. But it is true that I could never have done this without your help. We cannot have a renegade *ubiytsa* acting outside of ordered hits. It's unprofessional. For your assistance in taking Konrad down, the mafia will grant you unconditional protection beyond what even I can offer you alone. Katy, you will never have to fear anything or anyone ever again."

"I just thought I would feel worse about this," I admit.

"I know what you mean," he replies. "When I killed the men who murdered my mother and sister I feared that I would feel guilty. I feared that I would never wash the blood from my hands, that they'd be stained red for the rest of my life. I was afraid that their faces would haunt my dreams. But in the end, I was relieved. It felt like justice had finally been restored. I balanced the scales and set the world straight again. Perhaps it is a bizarre version of justice, but it is mine, and it is the code by which I live my life. I do not regret my choices, and neither should you."

"I don't regret it yet, but I feel like maybe it'll be a delayed reaction," I tell him honestly.

"Well, if it does hit you later and you start to feel

bad, come to me. I will make you feel right again, I promise. I will always make things better, however I can." He pauses to look at me as we stop at a red light. "Katy, our year together may have started under strange circumstances. I know that if things were different, we probably would never have met. But I want you to know that I have never done this before — any of this. And that it means something to me. *You* mean something to me."

His words send a happy shiver down my spine. Ivan is kind, he is devoted, but rarely is he so expressive with his emotions. I lift his hand and kiss each of his knuckles fondly. He gazes at me with his mouth parted slightly, his eyes roving over my face, focusing on my lips. Just that look is enough to make me wish we were already at the apartment. I want to crawl across the console and straddle him in the damn driver's seat.

The light turns green and we speed off immediately, breaking at least a few traffic laws to make the rest of the trip as brief as possible. Finally we screech to a stop outside the big marble building and before I can even unbuckle my seatbelt, Ivan has bounded out and around the car to open my door and pull me out. There, in the busy noonday streets of New York City, with the ever-present car horns and sirens in the distance, he sweeps me up into a deep, encompassing kiss. His hands reach around to wrap themselves in my hair, pulling me close. I know he is probably getting a little blood on my cheek from the slash down his face, but I don't care.

In fact, I don't care what else happens. All that matters right now is the handsome, impossibly strong man holding me in his arms. I want him to crush me into him, I want him to take me and make me forever his. Ivan is all that I need.

"This year has meant something to me, too," I tell him breathlessly between kisses. "Ivan, you mean everything to me."

He cups my face in both hands, staring into my eyes with that smoldering blue gaze. I want to kiss him endlessly, fall into his arms, into his warmth forever. I want him, all of him — the dark and the light.

"*Ya tebya lyublyu,*" he whispers, and I don't even have to ask what that means.

"I love you, too," I answer, without hesitation.

For the first time, I see a full, unabashed grin spread across his sharp features. This is a thousand-watt smile I have not seen the likes of before. He is a ray of radiant light, a pillar of noonday sun beamed into my world, and I suddenly cannot imagine a life without him in it.

I kiss him hard, with my emotions compelling my every movement. It feels like my skin is aflame — I am burning for him, to be near him, to be with him. I need him inside of me.

And it is evident that Ivan feels the same. He grasps me by the hand and pulls me out of the street, onto the pavement, and through the revolving doors. My coat billows out in the brisk air, nearly revealing my lingerie-clad body, but I can't bring myself to care at all. At this point, I would dance naked through the crowded streets of New York City just to follow Ivan anywhere he wanted to go. I would do anything.

We bolt through the lobby and I can't help but let out a peal of genuine laughter. Ivan glances back at me with a full-on grin and hurries me into the elevator.

As soon as the metal doors shut, he pushes me against the cold walls and pins my arms above my head, biting kisses into the flesh of my neck and collarbone. A long moan escapes my lips as my eyes roll toward heaven. He nudges my legs apart with his knee and rubs against me, his massive cock hard on my bare thigh. I want to fuck him here in the elevator, but too quickly there's a high-pitched ding, and the doors slide open again. Ivan hoists me into his arms and carries me bridal-style into his apartment, his lips locked with mine.

Before we even make it to the bedroom, he drapes me over the couch and jerks my legs open, hooking a finger under my panties to slide them out of the way. He drops to his knees and immediately plunges his tongue inside me, sucking at my clit and dragging his tongue up and down along my folds. I throw my head back and grip the edges of the couch to keep from falling off. Ivan isn't holding back in the least, devouring my pussy like a hungry animal.

"You're so wet for me," he growls from between my legs.

"I can't help myself," I reply, breathing hard.

"Neither can I," Ivan says. The next moment he eases a finger into my cunt, his tongue still lapping at my clit. He curls his finger up in a come-hither gesture inside of me, gently pumping back and forth, in and out. Each motion strokes that deep, forbidden part of me that sends my every nerve into overdrive. I can't stifle the cry of pleasure that erupts from my mouth when he speeds up, caressing my g-spot over and over again while his warm, wet tongue sucks up my juices and toys with my bud.

As I begin to rock against his face, riding the rhythm of his fingers and tongue working in tandem, he groans his satisfaction. The deep thrum of his voice through my pussy makes me shudder and clutch the couch as my first orgasm reaches its crest. I can feel the walls of my cunt contracting around Ivan's finger, but he doesn't ease up. I almost want to recoil from him, give my body a chance to recover, but Ivan isn't having any of that.

He tugs me closer to him, burying his face in my cunt, breathing in the scent of my sex and licking up my sweet honey as though it's the best thing he's ever had in his mouth. He speeds up his machinations, finger-fucking me hard and fast. My clit is so overstimulated that it almost hurts, but before long I feel another orgasm crashing down on me.

This time, Ivan merely lays his face on my exposed stomach and wraps his arms around me as I tremble through waves of overwhelming bliss, holding me tight. Then he stands up, pulls my panties down, and tosses them aside. He turns me around and takes my heavy coat, draping it over the back of the couch before he moves back to unhook my bra. My breasts fall free and he reaches around to hold them, massaging them gently in his large, calloused hands. He presses a kiss to the ticklish, bare skin of my neck.

"You are so beautiful, Katy," he murmurs. "I have never held such a lovely and delicate creature in my arms. I cannot wait to make you mine."

"Take me, please," I reply quietly, leaning back into him, letting myself fall limp in his strong, capable arms. Never have I felt so protected and safe and cherished. Adrenaline still prickles in my veins and it makes me feel bold, ravenous for him.

He leads me away into the bedroom, where he quickly undresses. He lifts me onto the bed, cradling my head as he lays me down amid a sea of blankets and pillows. Ivan climbs over me, kissing his way up my body, showering my exposed skin with bruising marks and delicate, feather-light pecks alike. I want to give him everything. I want so badly for him to peel me open like a flower, fill me up and make me feel whole.

Finally his lips find their way to mine and he kisses me deeply, his tongue exploring my mouth as he hands stroke my face, my hair. I know exactly what I want.

"Ivan," I murmur, "I need to feel you inside me. I want to be close to you."

He reaches down between my legs to stroke my clit, jolting me with a shock of pleasure.

"I want you," he says, "I want you forever, *mishka*."

"You can have me — everything, every part. I belong to you. Mafia or not, no matter what, I belong to you," I tell him, the words spilling freely from my mouth.

He rests his forehead against mine and whispers, "Katy, *lyubov moya*, I have been searching for so long to feel this way. Not since I first left Russia have I felt so secure, so complete. You make me feel like I am home again. No matter where I go, as long as you are beside me, I will be happy. You carry my home in your heart."

He kisses me once more and then he pulls back to position the head of his hard shaft against my eager opening. I roll my hips upward, urging him to hurry. So many emotions are coursing through my body and I need him now more than ever.

With a smile, he pushes inside of me, unprotected and uninhibited.

The sensation is magnificent. I feel so close to him as he pumps into me with abandon. I know he has been waiting for this moment for a long time, and I realize now that so have I.

"Oh, my angel," he groans, leaning forward to kiss my breasts, my neck, to bite my lips and whisper words I don't understand into my ear.

"Ivan, please," I whimper, my legs wrapping around his waist. "I need you."

He pushes into me hard, hitting that delicious place deep inside so that every thrust drives me closer and closer to another climax. I reach for him blindly, fumbling to pull him ever closer, to melt into him. I clench my pussy around his cock, rocking against his rhythmic thrusts, desperate to make him feel the same bliss that he gives me. And the look on his face tells me that I am succeeding.

"Please, I need you to fill me up," I croon.

"Are you sure?" he asks, but his eyes reveal how badly he wants it, too.

"More than ever," I reply assuredly.

And with that, with one final push, I scream out my orgasm and he follows suit, spilling his hot, precious seed inside of my hungry cunt. I clench my legs around him, clinging to every last drop of his honey. He kisses me with abandon, his hands brushing my hair out of my face, caressing my cheeks, stroking my arms, my waist.

For hours we stay in bed together, entwined in both lust and newfound love.

KATY

*E*ven if it was just a few months ago, all that feels like ancient history now. Finally, the longest year of my life with Ivan has come to an end.

And there's nowhere else I'd rather be than at his side.

Both of us are bundled up in heavy jackets as we crunch through the leaf-covered roads of the little country road we're taking a walk down. It's been our routine this past week, walking around and taking in the sights outside the little villa we rented outside Marseille, France.

I've always wanted to see Europe, but I thought that dream had been crushed when the mafia-run Amber Room fell into my lap. If I could go back in time and tell myself that mafia tie would end up sending me on a two-week vacation to the French countryside wrapped around the arm of the man of my dreams, I would have laughed in my own face.

But here I am, and I couldn't be happier!

Ivan's just as happy as I feel, too. As we make our way through the rustic scenery, where autumn is casting its blanket over the whole picturesque hillscape, I look up into his stormy blue eyes, and when he isn't looking lovingly back down at me, his gaze is roaming around the amber fields and forests with the same wonder I saw him looking at Central Park all those months ago. A lifetime ago.

Ivan has been paying for the whole trip, at his insistence, but thanks to how well the Amber Room has been doing, I could pay for a whole second trip, if I wanted to.

Business has been in full swing, and I haven't had to worry about a thing from the mob since Ivan and I fell in love.

Particularly since he put a diamond ring around my finger.

He proposed in Central Park, and even if it was just as corny as the first time he took me on a carriage ride there, I bawled my eyes out before hugging him tight and telling him I'd never let him go. Now, my club is mafia-protected in the truest way, and so am I.

I couldn't have taken this big of a vacation if it weren't for my incredible staff, either, and I haven't forgotten all their support in getting me where I am, either. As business picked up, so did my staff's paychecks, and Natalie has been training a crew of the best bartenders and servers Brighton Beach has ever seen.

That's not her only accomplishment in the past few months, either. Just before Ivan and I left for France, Natalie and Ashton took a day off to move into their new apartment together, and from what I hear, it's about twice the size of either of their old places.

I'm snapped out of my reminiscing by Ivan's voice.

"A carriage, I think."

"Hm?" I look up at him and tilt my head. He peers back down at me and smiles.

"That little cafe in the city I told you about this morning, I think it would be nice to take a carriage ride into town to enjoy the sights. Wouldn't want you tiring yourself out," he adds, extending his hand to rub my swollen stomach affectionately.

In fact, it's been about six months since Ivan and I shared a night together without protection, and to say I'm showing is putting it lightly. Ivan has been supporting me the whole time we've been on our walk.

An hour or so later, our carriage is rattling down the old stone roads towards Marseille, and I'm snuggled up against Ivan lovingly. His strong arms, hard and defined even through his autumn coat in what's turning out to be a chilly winter for France, make me feel as loved and protected as they did the first night I went home with him, when he was a total stranger I slept with before even knowing his name. It's so strange to think back to when I thought Ivan would just be a one-night fling, but I couldn't be happier for what it's become.

We sit in loving silence together, taking in the sights, sounds, and aromas of the fields around us when I finally break it with the news that's been in the back of my mind all morning.

"I think it's a boy, Ivan."

I feel him tense up in surprise at the sudden news, and it's followed by a tight squeeze closer to him as he beams down at me with adoration.

"Wh- are you sure? How do you know?"

"I just know," I say, cuddling tighter into his embrace. "And he'll be every bit as strong as you, I can feel it."

I feel his heart beat faster and his lips press against my forehead. He slips his hand around mine, and after a few moments adds, "I know you weren't so sure about a name before, have you...?"

"Henry," I say after a pause, "I think I want to name him Henry, after my dad." I've been conflicted about it over the past few days, thinking about names of any gender, but when I say it out loud, it feels right.

Ivan smiles warmly at me, and I know he feels the same. "Henry it is."

Now it's my turn to stretch myself up to kiss him, but he has to bend down a little to help me reach, and I end up giggling into his neck as we come closer, our lips pressing together and tongues delving into each other's mouths.

"Ivan," I finally say as we break the kiss, "It's been such a long year, and when this first started, there was nothing I wanted more for it to all be over. But now, it's like all the memories I really want to hold onto are the ones that happened after we met. There's nowhere I'd rather be than here with you, right now."

There's a tear in my eye at my own outpouring of emotion, and as Ivan looks down at me, he wipes them away with a finger.

"I feel the same, *mishka*. To tell you the truth," he twiddles the thumbs of those powerful, deadly hands, "I...I never realized it until sometime into our arrangement, but looking back on it," he looks up at me again with those eyes that hold so much tenderness in reserve for me alone, "I've loved you from the moment I laid eyes on you."

We move in simultaneously to press our lips together, and after we break, I bring my ruby-red lips to his ear and whisper, even as a smile tugs at my face.

"I think I'd like to renew our year together, my love. Make it a lifetime."

* * *

DON'T MISS out on the rest of the Hitman Series by Alexis Abbott! Now available on all ebook retailers.

Owned by the Hitman
Ebook | Audiobook | Paperback

Sold to the Hitman
Ebook | Audiobook | Paperback

Saved by the Hitman
Ebook | Paperback

Captive of the Hitman
Ebook | Paperback

Stolen from the Hitman
Ebook | Paperback

Hostage of the Hitman
Ebook | Paperback

Taken by the Hitman
Ebook | Paperback

ALSO BY ALEXIS ABBOTT

Romantic Suspense:

ALEXIS ABBOTT'S BOUND TO THE BAD BOY SERIES:

Book 1: Bound for Life

Book 2: Bound to the Mafia

Book 3: Bound in Love

ALEXIS ABBOTT'S HITMEN SERIES:

Owned by the Hitman

Sold to the Hitman

Saved by the Hitman

Captive of the Hitman

Stolen from the Hitman

Hostage of the Hitman

Taken by the Hitman

The Hitman's Masquerade (Short Story)

ROMANTIC SUSPENSE STANDALONES:

Criminal

Ruthless

Innocence For Sale: Jane

Redeeming Viktor

Sights on the SEAL

Rock Hard Bodyguard

Abducted

Vegas Boss

I Hired A Hitman

Killing For Her

The Assassin's Heart

Romance:

Falling for her Boss (Novella)

Most Wanted: Lilly (Novella)

Bound as the World Burns (SFF)

Erotic Thriller:

THE DANGEROUS MEN SERIES:

The Narrow Path

Strayed from the Path

Path to Ruin

ABOUT THE AUTHOR

Alexis Abbott is a Wall Street Journal & USA Today bestselling author who writes about bad boys protecting their girls! Pick up her books today if you can't resist a bad boy who is a good man, and find yourself transported with super steamy sex, gritty suspense, and lots of romance.

She lives in beautiful St. John's, NL, Canada with her amazing husband.

CONNECT WITH ALEXIS

Want to keep up to date with Alexis Abbott's new releases, sales, and giveaways? Want a **Free** bad boy romance novel? Subscribe to Alexis' VIP Reader List: http://alexisabbott.com/newsletter

facebook.com/abbottauthor

twitter.com/abbottauthor

instagram.com/alexisabbottauthor

bookbub.com/authors/alexis-abbott

pinterest.com/badboyromance